NEVER SAY NEVER

McLaughlin Brothers, Book 3

JENNIFER ASHLEY

JA / AG Publishing

Chapter One

Brooke

CRAP. He's here.

Austin McLaughlin strolls into my showroom like he owns the place. Sauntering, exuding confidence, jerking his chin at my lead salesman who moves to intercept him.

Austin says a few words I can't hear and Mike grins, then motions him to me.

I'm at my standing desk in the back, facing the showroom, to go over paperwork. I'm clearly busy, but Austin strides for me like I have all the time in the world to speak with him.

I would for any other client. But this is Austin McLaughlin.

Once upon a time—or a year and a half ago—I dated him. Okay, *dated* is a tame word for what we had. It was wild, insane, fun, frustrating, infuriating ...

And then it was over. We walked away from each other, for many reasons.

I hadn't seen Austin until a few months ago, at my friend Calandra's wedding. Calandra married the oldest McLaughlin brother, and I was a bridesmaid, so of course I had to deal with Austin being there.

He'd pretended to ignore me, so I pretended to ignore him. He'd continued like this at my friend Abby's wedding rehearsal—she's marrying another McLaughlin, and again, I'm a bridesmaid.

After that rehearsal dinner, more than a week ago, I found myself alone with him, entirely by accident. Maybe Austin knew I'd been sitting in that courtyard behind the restaurant—maybe he didn't.

Whatever. We'd had a stilted discussion. I'd forced myself to talk business when he'd mentioned his dream of owning a great car. I'd even encouraged him to drop in and test one of our vehicles. I could be civil, couldn't I? And maybe make a commission on top of it.

I didn't think Austin would come so soon. I also didn't think he'd ask for me. We have plenty of competent salespeople here, including Mike, who's very good. I don't need to give Austin hands-on service.

Why does my blood heat when I think of *hands-on service?*

Probably because he's better looking than he needs to be in his casual shirt and wind-mussed hair. Austin moves in his slow, self-assured way past a Lamborghini and an Aston Martin without seeming to notice them.

His gaze is fixed on me, his dark blue eyes as sexy as ever.

Austin says nothing when he reaches me. I don't like him standing so close, even though my desk is between us. He reaches into my personal space somehow. Part of me wants to run. The other part? It wants to rush around the desk and stand even closer.

"Can I help you?" I give him my chirpy greeting, pretending he's just another customer.

"Taking you up on your offer."

The way Austin says the words, with his hint of smile, puts plenty of double-entendre into the sentence. Triple-entendre even.

"To show you our cars," I say firmly. I'm all business, me.

"Sure." Austin rests his hands on the desk, arms apart, which makes his muscles knot. I have a flash of how I used to stroke my fingers up and down those muscles, and I suck in a breath.

"I'm not certain it's a good move for me," Austin continues. "But I might be convinced."

I'm not certain talking to him is a good move for *me*. However, this is a car business, and my job is to sell cars. High-dollar luxury cars, which people don't buy every day. The average driver regards cars as transportation. Something nice, yes, with as many bells and whistles as possible for their buck, but affordable. Most people have a budget.

Luxury and fantasy car buyers are different. They also have a budget, but they are more interested in a certain model or a limited edition and will be somewhat flexible with price in order to purchase.

The men—and plenty of women too—who walk in here are excited about cars. It's fun to sell to them, because they truly love them. They appreciate every aspect.

I fall into salesperson mode. "We talked about a starter car, one to introduce you without shocking your wallet. I mentioned a Maserati."

Austin drives a Merc sports car that's plenty flashy if a low-end commercial model, and his eyes light when I mention the Maserati. He's interested. This encounter could lead to a sale ... or it could lead to me regretting I ever spoke to him at Abby's rehearsal dinner.

I make myself smile. "All right. Follow me."

Austin's near grin becomes a full one. I expect him to give me an Austin comeback, like *I'll follow you anywhere, sweetheart.* But he simply nods and skims around the desk as I go to the coded lock box and remove a set of keys.

I lead him through a back door to a walled lot behind the showroom. We don't keep the hugely expensive cars on the premises—the vehicles in the showroom and most in the gated back lot are demo models.

The Maserati I lead Austin to is one of the few we stock for immediate sale. It's a black Ghibli, with hand-stitched leather seats and carbon-fiber trims. Austin's smile fades as he scans it, interest lighting his face.

"That is one cool automobile," he says, sounding reverent.

"An intro car, but it has all the fine features Maserati puts into every vehicle."

"Stop talking like a commercial and tell me about this car. It's awesome."

"How about you find out for yourself?" I dangle a key fob. "Drive it."

"Hot damn." Austin closes his fingers around the fob.

In the instant before I drop it into his palm, a spark leaps from him to me, just as it had when I'd handed him my business card after the rehearsal dinner.

Our eyes meet. Austin has very black lashes, a good contrast with his blue eyes. I'd never been attracted to blue-eyed men until I met Austin. Never since either.

He turns away, pretending no fires have singed us. He opens the door and slides into the driver's seat. I hurry around the car and enter the passenger side.

Austin settles in, wriggling a little as the soft leather cups his body. He adjusts the mirror and inhales. "Love that new car smell."

"Start it up," I say encouragingly.

Austin lifts the key then realizes the car has a push-button starter. He clicks it, and the engine purrs to life.

"Sweet." His smart-ass expression fades. I know he didn't come here to buy a car—he wants to annoy me ... but now he's realizing how much he likes this Ghibli.

I click a remote I carry in my pocket and the back gate slowly rolls open. "Take her out."

Austin revs the engine, which has a throaty but almost velvety purr. Lots of power, but it doesn't need to show off.

"Feels good." Austin again moves in the seat, and my skin tingles. I want to wriggle too, remembering his body covering mine in the dark, his warmth, his slow kisses. *You feel good,* he would whisper.

Palms sweating, I shake off the memory with effort.

Austin scans the dashboard, pushes all the buttons, familiarizes himself with the car. He uses controls to adjust the mirror, the seat, the steering wheel. Last he plays with the sound system, scanning the satellite radio to find a station he likes.

Dance music flows through the car, and Austin rocks to it. "Mind? Can't drive a piece like this without a good beat."

Not waiting for my answer, he pulls through the gate to the narrow lane outside, singing along with the song.

I raise my voice to be heard. "It's like you're fifteen."

At least Austin doesn't tear out, squealing the tires as I half expect him to. He's careful—this is about a hundred grand worth of car.

"Nuh-uh. If I'd driven a thing like this with a hot girl next to me when I was fifteen, with no license, I would have got my ass whooped."

From his mother, he meant, who would have blown a gasket. His dad would have given him a stern but quiet talking to. Not that his mom would have hit him, but Austin would have been grounded forever.

"By the way, how are your parents?" I ask.

We reach Colter, and he turns west, the street leading to quiet neighborhoods.

"They're great." Austin rests one hand easily on the wheel, the other arm on the console between us. "They're thrilled they have two sons married off, another engaged, and a grandkid on the way. The old homestead will be inundated with babies before long."

"Not a bad thing." I've been to Austin's parents' house plenty of times, and it's a place made for kids.

"Didn't say it was. They'll be cute as hell, and I can teach them how to gang up on their dads." Austin laughs in delighted anticipation. "How's your family?"

They miss Austin, but I'm not about to tell him that. "Good." I shrug. "You know. Getting through life. My brother just got a promotion."

"Cedric did? Awesome. He deserves it. Tell him that."

I picture my older brother, a big guy, easy-going, deep-voiced, quiet, who was smarter than anyone gave him credit for. He's an architect at a firm where you have to sacrifice blood to move up the ladder. Austin and I first connected through him, when the McLaughlins were looking for an architect for help in their home-building charity, and Calandra suggested Cedric. I'd known the McLaughlins through Calandra, but mostly only Ryan, the guy she married.

Austin had come to see Cedric a day I'd also stopped by Cedric's office, and the rest is history.

We drive through neighborhoods, Austin going carefully. Signs here and there proclaim "No test driving"—there are a number of dealerships nearby—and Austin avoids those streets.

We emerge onto wider avenues, where traffic is sparse this Sunday afternoon. Austin lets the car go faster, grinning as the engine rumbles.

"Would love to take this on the open road." His eyes gleam.

"Not today." Of course Austin would want to take it for a real drive, but there's only so much we can do within the city. "We have a track, where you can really see what it can do. I can make you an appointment."

"Sounds good. Set it up."

Austin is confident, as he is all the time. He takes delight in everything, no inhibitions.

I watch his hands resting lightly on the wheel, and have another flash of memory. Austin lying beside me in my bed in a pool of sunshine, those hands brushing my skin, his slow smile as he leans to kiss me.

I suck in a breath, my heart on fire. For an instant I *feel* him, remember the excitement he built in me. I miss it. Life—my personal, non-work life—has been flat since we broke up.

"You okay?" Austin glances at me then fixes his eyes on traffic again.

"Yes." I force myself to calm. "Just fine."

"My driving's not worrying you?"

"No. You've always been a good driver."

Which is true. Austin takes care of his cars and isn't reckless. He likes to see what any vehicle can do, but he's not a daredevil.

A man idles next to us, admires the Maserati, and gives Austin a thumbs-up. Austin returns the gesture.

The light changes, and Austin glides the car smoothly along. "Wow, I think you just gave me a compliment."

"I did. Suck it up."

He chuckles, the gravelly laugh I used to love. "I will accept and keep the compliment. Maybe take it out and stroke it every once in a while."

More heat crawls along my skin. I have to stop this.

"We should head back." I keep my voice as nonchalant as possible. "If you're interested, I can reserve this one for you, or you can come back and do the track drive if you're not sure."

"Hmm." Austin pulls around an SUV and makes a turn to the street that leads to our back lot. "I might have to takes several more test drives. See if I really like it."

I roll my eyes. "Sure, Austin. Like every day for the next year?"

"Hey, that sounds good. I'll take you up on that."

My quick temper surges. "I—"

Austin bursts out laughing. "You are way too easy to tease. Always were."

"Do you want the car or not?" My voice sounds harsh, but only because he's making me nervous.

Austin gives me a wide-eyed stare. "How many high-dollar cars do you sell with that kind of sales pitch? What happened to coaxing and persuading?"

"You're not a real customer. You came to look at this car to mess with me, didn't you?"

Am I disappointed? Or happy to be with him again? I can't tell, so I keep my frown in place.

Austin whistles. "Your ego hasn't shrunk. I truly am interested in the car. How cool would it be to own and drive this? You asked me not to go to another dealer when we talked at the rehearsal dinner, which was fair, so here I am." His offended expression fades and his lips twitch. "But I can't help messing with you a *little* bit."

He never could. "All right then. Do we start the order when we get to the showroom? Or do you walk away? It's a sweet deal." I try to soften my tone—a sale is never a bad thing.

Austin taps the steering wheel, as though he's thinking. The gates of our dealership are coming up.

"Tell you what." He slows the car as the gate rolls back, but he pauses instead of pulling inside. "I'll take this car—only from you ... if you'll go out with me."

Chapter Two

____

Austin

BROOKE STARES at me as though I just proposed we smash this beautiful automobile right into the wall.

Her dark brows draw down even more over her amazing brown eyes, and she gets ready to tell me to go to hell.

"For coffee," I say hastily. My brothers would laugh at how fast I backpedal, but I'm not letting this opportunity go. "You can tell me more about the car and why I should buy it."

She hesitates. Brooke doesn't trust me, and I don't blame her.

"I promise." I lift my hands. "Coffee. Speech. You can sit on the far side of the table. This is a big decision for me. I love this car, obviously, but it's a huge commitment."

Brooke's face softens. I see a humorous glint in her

eye, and I expect her to make a crack about me and commitment, but she nods once.

"Okay. But I'm driving in *my* car, and I pick the place."

"All absolutely fine with me." I pull in through the gates, which roll shut.

I'm sorry to park the Ghibli and turn it off. I've not driven something this fine before, and everything in me cries out for it.

But another part of me is dancing like a maniac, because Brooke said yes to the date. I mean coffee—just coffee. Not a date.

I try not to spin on my toes like my brother Ben's dancer fiancée, but it's tough. My heels have wings as we walk back into the showroom.

Brooke is now part-owner of this dealership, and she can take off whenever she wants to sweet-talk a customer into a purchase. She tells Mike, who seems like a nice guy, that she's gone for the day, and he bids her a cheerful good-night.

We step out into heat. It's after six in the evening, but in June that means temperatures lingering into the hundreds. The sun is bright and we slam on sunglasses against it.

Brooke drives an older model Aston Martin that she obviously bought from the dealership. Sleek and sporty, it fits her. She keeps it locked in one of the garages, and a mechanic polishing one of the other vehicles inside gives her a wave.

The car windows are tinted enough that it shields

the worst of the sun, plus the car is cool from sitting in the garage all day. Comfortable.

Brooke says nothing as she pulls out of the dealership, more gestures of farewell from the guys who work there. They like her, I can see, and not only because she's a beautiful woman. There's respect and warmth in their smiles. I'm glad for her, knowing how she struggled to achieve that respect.

The coffee house Brooke drives us to is five minutes away, on Camelback. I'd hoped for a longer time to talk to her, but we arrive before I can think of a conversation starter.

"Oh damn." Brooke parks the car in front of the coffee house and gazes in dismay at the door. "Closed at six." It's six-thirty.

"We can try somewhere else." I glance down the row of shops in the strip mall and focus on one at the end—a wine bar. Even better. "That place is open." I point.

Brooke cranes her head. "I've never tried it."

"Looks popular." The cars in this lot are clustered around the front door. "Plus we're already here."

Brooke shrugs and shuts off her car. I don't bother to try to run around to open her door for her—she'll scowl at me and think I'm up to something. I want this to be a casual outing. Just friends.

As I let Brooke precede me down the walk, my gaze is drawn to the curve of her hips, the beauty of her legs as she strides. She's wearing a tawny brown dress, businesslike and not too tight, her arms and legs bare for the heat. A pair of gold sandals with low heels complement the dress.

Brooke's skin is dark, her black hair a satin wave. She sometimes streaks it blue, or red, but today it's all her own color.

I get caught in looking at her, my pulse speeding, and then we're at the door. I take a few quick steps and open it for her—I can take the friendship thing only so far. Besides, I hold the door for any lady, including my sisters-in-law and my mom. Brooke glances at me but doesn't seem displeased.

I follow Brooke into a dark interior with bare wood tables and a polished wooden bar across the far wall. I enjoy a good wine, and Brooke does too. It's one of the things we bonded over when we first went out.

"Good evening." A chipper maître d' in a suit greets us. "Welcome. I haven't seen you here before."

"First time for everything," I say lightly.

"I'm sorry—do we need a reservation?" Brooke glances around. The tables are mostly full, with couples or groups of friends talking, relaxing.

"Not at all," the maître d' says quickly. "Friday and Saturday, yes, but other nights we can accommodate walk-in guests. Is this table all right?" He pauses by one near the door. "The sommelier will be with you, or you can order at the bar."

"Thank you—the table is fine." Brooke turns on her smile for the maître d', who is floored. That smile melts all before her, including me.

I hold out the chair for Brooke. Again, nothing I

wouldn't do for my sisters-in-law. Brooke says not a word as she sinks gracefully into it, sliding her purse under the table. I take the seat across from her, and my backside barely touches the chair before the sommelier is beside us with an open bottle and two tasting glasses.

"This is the recommended vintage tonight." He trickles wine into the glasses. "But of course, peruse the menu and ask me any questions. I want to pair you with the right wine."

I lift the glass and hold it to my chin and then just under my nose. It's a red with a deep color, good legs, and a mellow, berry scent. Brooke does the same, sipping before I do.

Her eyes glow with pleasure. "Very nice," she says.

I sip. The wine is dark and fruity, quite smooth. It was a French wine, I guessed, a Syrah, possibly a blend. "Agree. How about a bottle of this?"

Brooke nods, and the sommelier, pleased, glides away to fetch one for us.

"It's lovely." Brooke rolls the last drops of wine around her glass. "I never realized this place was here. I like the coffee house and never turned my head to see what was nearby."

"You're focused." I lean back in my chair. "One thing I always liked about you."

"Right. I remember us yelling about that."

"Only when you got *too* focused." I flex my shoulders and set down my glass, lounging in the chair. I want to keep this relaxed. "Bygones."

Brooke is about to answer when the sommelier

returns. The wine is indeed a Syrah from the northern Rhone Valley, and I'm pleased with myself for guessing that. Brooke and I had taken a wine course together in Napa—I still had part of the case of wine from that sojourn. The wine lasted longer than our relationship.

The sommelier lets me taste first, to make sure the bottle is all right, then when I give him a nod, he fills both glasses and leaves the bottle on a stand next to the table. A waiter brings us snacks—crackers, fruit, and cheese—along with plates, cutlery, and napkins.

By the time this flurry settles and the servers withdraw, Brooke has loosened, the lines around her mouth smoothing out.

I lift my glass. "To great cars."

"I'll drink to that." She clicks her glass to mine, and we take a moment to truly enjoy the wine.

"Have you heard from Abby and Zach at all?" Brooke asks. She leans back in her seat, one hand resting loosely on the table, the other fingering her glass.

"The honeymooners?" The wedding last weekend passed off without a hitch. I'd managed to avoid Brooke, and she'd managed to avoid me. My brother Zach shoved aside his bachelorhood and looked happy as hell about it. "No. Are you kidding? They're enjoying the cool weather of Santa Fe, hiking and shit like that." *When they remember to leave the bedroom, that is,* I add silently.

"I'm glad for Abby. I remember Zach coming downstairs the day after Calandra and Ryan's wedding, pretending so hard he wasn't looking for Abby. Failed miserably." Brooke laughs, the silken sound I've missed so much. "I gave him her number. I felt sorry for him."

"Yeah? I didn't hear you'd done that." Zach had mentioned he'd seen Brooke that morning, but not that she'd given him Abby's number. Zach had been pining, that was for sure. "Good for you."

"They needed to get together. Same with Calandra and Ryan."

I grimace. "Don't remind me. Ryan was a serious headache. Ben, I'm happy to say, is much more sensible. He's madly in love with Erin and is rolling with it."

"I really like Erin." Brooke nods her approval. "Just the woman Ben needs."

"Yep. Everyone's paired off. I'm the only one left."

"That's true." Brooke takes a sip of wine. "I wonder why that is? Oh, I remember. You're a pain in the ass."

I pretend her comment doesn't sting. "I like to think of myself as *quirky*. I'll be the crazy bachelor uncle who lets the kids get away with shit their parents don't, and take them for drives in my awesome Maserati."

"Sounds like you're interested in the car."

"Amazing how quick you're back on topic. Of course I'm interested in the car. Who wouldn't be?" I fold my arms on the table. "What can you offer me?"

I mean about financing the vehicle, of course, but Brooke's eyes narrow a tad. I watch her decide to let the possible double-meaning go.

"I can write it up for you tomorrow. Down

payment, credit checks, that sort of thing. Get the paperwork ready."

Down payment. For a car like that it will be a huge amount in order for a bank to finance little old me and not make the monthly payments more than my salary. "Let me check my accounts, and I'll see what I can come up with."

I don't need to check, actually. I know exactly how much I have in my bank accounts—checking, savings, retirement account Mom insisted on setting up for each of us.

"You can always lease," Brooke suggests.

"I don't know. A car like that." I shake my head. "I'd hate to give it back at the end of the term." The statement makes me remember how I'd had to give up Brooke, and regret touches me.

She shrugs, oblivious to my thoughts. "It's an option."

While I'd driven the Ghibli, I'd visualized it as mine, but now I'm wondering if I can afford the damned thing at all. I already have a perfectly good car —a Mercedes C-class 300, which I've paid off, and it's a nice ride. I'm dreaming.

But if I say no and walk away, I won't have this precious time with Brooke. She'll finish her glass of wine, tell me to call a taxi or ride-share, and leave.

"Why don't you write it up either way?" I say. "I can look at all the numbers and decide which way to go." I wonder if her dealership takes trade-ins, but I'll broach that subject later.

"Sure, I can do that."

"Meanwhile ..." I lift the bottle and top off her glass. "Tell me more about the car and why I need it."

I'm sure she'll catch on to what I'm doing and tell me she has to go, but Brooke sits back, sips, and starts to talk about the Ghibli. What it can do, what I'll like about it.

She knows a lot about cars, more than anyone I've ever met. When she runs out of information about the Maserati, I ask her about the others I'd seen in her showroom—the Lamborghini and the Aston Martin. More incredible vehicles I'd love to drive.

Brooke knows all about engine specs, and not only that, she understands how the cars feel when they're on the road. Anyone can quote numbers from a book, but she describes how the motor sounds and its smoothness, how different cars handle in their own way, on a track versus the streets.

She's good. By the time the bottle is half empty— most of it drunk by me—I'm convinced I need to own the Maserati.

Brooke and I have so much in common—we appreciate good wine, classy automobiles, fun clubs, and great restaurants. My guy friends like cars and clubs too, but wine to most of them is bad grape juice and no substitution for a good beer. I enjoy beer as well, but many of them pour a keg down their throats for the buzz, not caring what the brew tastes like.

Then again, most of my guy friends, including my brothers, have now ceased partying. They caught the woman of their dreams and are married, some of them with little kids now. They no longer spend money on fast cars and tons of beer, instead going for the diapers on sale at the big discount stores. They're proud dads, and I'm happy for them, but my friends have a different focus now. My brothers are quickly moving in their direction.

Brooke is single, no guy in her life right now. I know this because Calandra and Abby talk about Brooke all the time in front of me. If Brooke was going out with someone, I'd know.

I'm single too, another thing we have in common. I dated a couple of women a year after Brooke and I ended things, but the relationships fizzled before they started. It's always been Brooke for me.

The evening meanders. I finish the bottle, and the good sommelier brings us another.

Brooke keeps herself to another half-glass, as she's driving, but she's loosened up, talking easily. Not as intimately as we used to, but enough to remind me why I always loved spending time with her.

We discuss my brothers marrying her friends and how things are going at McLaughlin Renovations. She tells me how she bought a half share in her business.

"You remember that Raymond didn't think I had anything inside my head," she says with a laugh. Raymond Bromley is the original owner of the dealership. "He wanted me to smile and flatter and talk men into putting huge amounts of money down for our cars. Took him a while to realize I had a knack for the business. You know, the reason I graduated top of my class with an MBA."

"I don't know—you've smiled, flattered, and talked me into saying yes to this Maserati." I lift my glass. "Plus have me half sauced."

"You did the half-sauced thing yourself, and I haven't flattered you into wanting the car. You're convinced because you know it's good."

"Yep." I toast her and drink. "You're one hell of a sales manager. Glad your idiot boss finally realized that. I knew he would."

I close my mouth quickly. It's a touchy subject, but Brooke continues as though I didn't bring up bad memories.

"Oh, Raymond's not so bad. Just grew up in a different era. When he started talking about selling the business, he was thrilled when I stepped up and made an offer. He loves that dealership and didn't want to see it in the hands of someone who wouldn't treasure it."

"You'll be awesome." I'm mellow and happy. "Just as you are at everything else."

Brooke regards me quizzically. "You told me today I had an ego. Why are you feeding it?"

"Because it's true that you're awesome. You are the most amazing woman I've ever met. No lie."

Her eyes tighten. "Stop."

"Why? Can't I give you compliments? I'm obviously not trying to get you into bed. That's over for us."

A profound sadness floods me as I say this, and I strive to keep it from showing on my face.

Do her lips twitch downward, as though she's sad too? Or is it wishful thinking?

I make my voice light. "Amazing and beautiful. Yeah, more compliments. Deal with it."

Her smile briefly flashes over her face and is gone. Brooke has always been dedicated to her work, but I see an emptiness in her, which I know can't be because of losing me.

Not that she lost me. I'm still around.

The second bottle is empty, and now I'm woozy. "I have to work in the morning. Mom will not be happy if I come in hungover."

"This is an excellent wine." Brooke turns the bottle in its stand and studies the label. "A very good wine won't give you a hangover, as long as you drink no other alcohol tonight."

"And *do* drink lots and lots of water. Not a problem. I want water in this heat anyway." I flag down a waiter and ask for the bill. He slides away to fetch it.

Brooke lifts her purse, and I put my hand on hers.

What previously jumped between us through business cards and keys is nothing to what ignites during our hand-to-hand touch. The contact fires up my body, burning away most of the alcohol.

Brooke's eyes widen, and she yanks her hand back.

"This is my treat," I say.

She's already shaking her head. "This is a business thing. You're a client. I pay."

"Old friends reconnecting," I counter. "My way of saying thank you for talking to me again."

"Bygones ..." Brooke ceases rummaging in her purse and fixes me with worried brown eyes. "Isn't that what you said?"

"Yeah, but we had some intense bygones." I have my card out by the time the waiter returns and I toss it to the tray without looking at the bill.

Brooke contemplates me a moment, her fingers tense. Then she releases her purse and sits back. "Okay. Thank you."

"My pleasure." I try to make the words polite, neutral, but it's so hard to be neutral with her. My emotions are jumping around all over the place.

The waiter returns and I sign the bill. It's high, but worth it to have this time with Brooke.

The sun has gone down when we emerge from the wine bar, and it's marginally cooler.

"I've had way too much to drink to drive home," I say as we approach her car. "Would you mind dropping me at my house? I'll pick up my car tomorrow, and you can show me how much money I'm handing you for the Ghibli."

Brooke moves hesitantly to the driver's side, keys in hand. I stand at the passenger door, holding my breath.

She's going to tell me to get a cab, and she'll see me later. She'll drive away, leaving me standing in the parking lot like a huge loser. I see the idea go through her head as she avoids looking at me directly.

Then Brooke heaves a sigh. "Get in."

Not the most promising invitation, but it's a start.

Too bad I live so close to this place. All of us

brothers like Central Phoenix, and we work in a home renovation business, so we each purchased a house in the area and went to work rebuilding it. Zach has an old craftsman bungalow, Ben took a very plain cinderblock home and transformed it, and Ryan bought his bride a Mission Revival cottage with a deep front porch.

I like a challenge, so I found a house up for auction that no one wanted—I was the only one who bothered to show up to bid on it. A small mid-century brick house, with two floors, in a historic neighborhood just north of Camelback. I couldn't change it too much because the district wants to keep the historic flavor, but the guys who work for McLaughlin Renovations know how to blend old and new to make it livable and retain the house's intrinsic beauty.

The only drawback is that it's about ten minutes from where we are now. Not enough time for me to continue our conversation and convince Brooke we should see each other again. You know, as friends.

Too soon, Brooke is pulling up in front of my house. We were together when I bought the place, and she remembers my struggles to make it perfect.

Does Brooke glance at the house in regret? Longing to see it one more time? She's always liked my home. Or is this wishful thinking again?

Brooke sets the brake. "Well, good night," she says. "See you tomorrow to go over paperwork. Say on your lunch hour?"

I'd planned to wait until six and come up with an excuse to maybe take her back to the wine bar or out to dinner. A quick drop-by during working hours is not what I have in mind.

"Sure," I make myself say. I open the door and climb out, then find myself against the car, my legs wobbling. "Hmm. Might need a little help here."

Brooke is already out and at my side. She slides her arm around me in exasperation. "I'm dumping you on your doorstep. Not putting you to bed."

"That's what you always say." I allow the teasing note, the grin. She's tucked me in before, lying down beside me to make all the pain go away.

"Nope. Front door." Brooke helps me hobble up the walk.

I have a nice yard with old growth trees lending shade, benches here and there to take advantage of said shade. The porch runs the length of the house, with chairs placed so my brothers can come over and drink beer when they want.

I drag out my keys and try to climb the porch steps at the same time. Bad idea.

I sag against Brooke. She half lifts me up the stairs and pushes me to lean against the door while she takes the keys and unlocks it for me.

"Hey." My voice is quiet as she starts to turn away. "Thank you."

The porch light is off, because I hadn't planned to stay out after dark. Moonlight touches Brooke's face, sculpting her in beauty.

I brush her cheek with the backs of my fingers. I

expect her to jerk away, but she takes a breath, stilling. Encouraged, I caress her again.

We've stood like this so many times, on this very porch, touching, kissing, and then I'd ask her in. I'd been ready to give her her own key, right before we broke up.

"A shame," I whisper.

She remains close to me. "What is?"

"So many things." I give up on constraint. I lean to Brooke, my beautiful lady, and gently press a kiss to her lips.

Her mouth goes still under my touch. Not rejecting me, but not welcoming either. The pain in my heart increases.

Then Brooke grabs the lapels of my shirt, drags me against her, and deepens the kiss into a passionate and yearning one.

Chapter Three

Brooke

OH, shit, what the hell am I doing? I'm kissing Austin McLaughlin and loving every second of it.

I should tear myself away and run like hell, but Austin's arms come around me, and my treacherous body relaxes against him.

He tastes of fine wine and a darkness that's all his own. His lips are firm and gentle at the same time, his kiss caressing even as it opens my mouth.

No hesitation from Austin. He wants to kiss me, and he's doing it thoroughly.

My legs are shaking, the space between my thighs hot with wanting. I step against him—I can't help it, and wrap my arms around him. His hands stroke my hair, the touch I miss so much. Austin's hands are skilled, magical.

I know that if he invites me inside I'll go without

vacillating. It feels good to have him against me again, all our harsh words melting into the darkness and the dry wind.

He makes a low sound in his throat, and I gasp. He jumps, and we break apart at the same instant.

We stare at each other, his eyes glistening. His chest rises swiftly, and I'm breathing hard too.

"I ..." My voice falters, cracking.

"No, don't say anything." The words are soft, holding a tender and urgent note. Austin reaches a hand toward me.

I duck away, my heart pounding. "I have to go." Lame, but that's all I can say. "Paperwork. Tomorrow. Good night."

I turn on my heel. I try for a dignified exit, but I trip on the stairs, my sandal twisting. I bite back a cry.

Austin is there to keep me from falling, holding me with his strength. I want to sink into him and stay with him all night.

Because I do, I wrench myself away. "No. Going. Now."

My speech is garbled, and I nearly run down the rest of the steps toward my car.

"Brooke." My name floats into the night, and everything inside me wants to respond, to dash back to him. "Wait ..."

I can't look at him, can't answer. If I do, I *will* stay, and we'll regret it. We'll rip the lid off what we closed, and all the bad will come pouring out, clogging up the peace I've finally found for myself.

Is it peace, a little voice asks me. *Or inertia?*

"Brooke ..."

It's hard to resist Austin's smooth tones, the promise as he says my name. I click my key fob about five times before my shaking fingers can make it unlock the door. I dive inside the car and start it, revving it with a nervous foot.

I see Austin in the middle of the walk as I pull away, watching me go. Not trying to stop me, not waving me off. Just standing in the dark.

Tears blur my eyes. "Damn it. *Damn* it."

I'd woken up so calm this morning. Had a busy, productive, and predictable day. Then Austin had to walk in.

Now my body is vibrant, something inside me rejoicing. I feel his kiss on my lips, Austin against me. I fit with him, our bodies locking so easily.

I pull onto Central, but the tears cloud my vision, so I veer off into a parking lot. The bulk of a church rises against the sky, its mid-century modern steeple pointing to heaven.

I rest my forehead on the steering wheel and sob.

I DIDN'T DRINK ENOUGH THE NIGHT BEFORE TO BE hung over—as I'd told Austin, a good wine shouldn't do that—but in the morning, my eyes are bloodshot and my body feels hollow.

Concealer helps hide the circles under my eyes, but

makeup can only do so much. When I walk into the dealership, dressed as smartly as I can, Mike takes one look at me and raises his brows.

"Rough night?" He hands me my mug filled with coffee. "Or a good one?"

I snatch the mug and dump hot liquid down my throat. "No different from any other night."

"Really? You left with a guy you used to go out with, and his car's still in the lot." Mike waves his cup at the glass door in the rear of the showroom. I see a slice of Austin's gray convertible through it.

"What makes you think I used to go out with him?" I snap. "And is that any way to talk to your boss?"

Mike and I have been friends since he started at the dealership a year ago. He's one of the few men who accepted me as an equal right away and never treated me like eye candy hired to entice males to part from their cash.

His smile flashes. "Sorry, boss. I noticed the tension between you two, and I just thought ... But I'm glad to see you cut loose—I mean, enjoy yourself. All work and no play ..."

"There was no play." I gulp more coffee. "I had a few glasses of wine, and I drove Austin home because he drank the other bottle and a half. I dropped him off and left. He's coming in to pick up his car today. I'll need comparison write-ups on the Ghibli—lease versus buying, plus the different specs on various down payments. By lunch, please."

Mike isn't deterred. "Sure thing, boss. Hope you land the sale."

"Just let me know when he comes in."

I'm usually not this crabby, but my head aches—not from a hangover but from lack of sleep. I'd lain awake most of the night, reliving our kiss.

Austin always kisses like he means it. No rushing, no mind on other things, no obvious hoping the kiss will lead to something more. He kisses as though he has all night, like the best thing he can possibly do at the moment is taste my lips.

He begins slowly, a soft pressure, before coaxing me to open to him. He eases my lips apart and then brushes my tongue with his, hot friction that awakens all my desires.

I can still feel his body against mine, strong arms cradling me like he'll protect me from the world. I could plaster myself against Austin for a long, long time, imbibing him and enjoying.

I might have run like hell last night, but I couldn't get him out of my head. Austin had stayed with me well into the morning, though he'll never know that.

Plunging into work will erase Austin from my brain, I tell myself, but I know better. That's like trying to forget I need food. Just when I distract myself from it, up pops the craving, and the very thing I don't want to think about dances before my eyes.

Doesn't help that I picture Austin dancing *naked.*

Austin has always been a goof, and one night, he'd sashayed around his bedroom, wriggling his bare hips to a bouncing song, singing at the top of his voice. I'd laughed so hard and realized how much I loved him.

Shit. I cut off that thought abruptly. Falling in love with Austin had been a big, big mistake.

The clock moves slowly today, and yet it doesn't. Too soon, it's approaching the lunch hour. Mike sells a car in the morning and I spend a welcome amount of time going through the paperwork. The buyer is a new customer. One of our repeat buyers recommended the dealership to him, which makes me happy. Nothing beats word of mouth.

At 11:30, Raymond Bromley, who owns half the business, appears. Nearing retirement, he leaves the day-to-day running of the place to me, which suits me fine.

"I've been on the phone all morning with Simon Lethbridge," Raymond says. "He's finally decided to take the Lamborghini."

"Excellent." I perk up, trying to brush away the nervousness about Austin's imminent arrival. "How long have we been trying to convince him?"

Raymond considers, his silver hair catching a glint of sunlight. "Three months? I know he's careful, but ..."

Simon Lethbridge is a British man who'd relocated to Arizona to live in a place without rain. Well, we have rain at times, but not like they do in England. He inherited gobs of money from a family who'd owned about ten businesses and stays in any place in the world he wants, for as long as he wants, though he doesn't part with his money easily.

He likes cars, however, and often comes to the showroom to browse. He'd purchased a Bentley from us a couple years ago but said he wanted something more sporty just for fun. Simon had finally started getting serious, narrowing down what he wanted with my help, but he'd been dragging his feet about making a final choice.

"There's a catch." Raymond stuffs his hands in the pockets of his slacks and eyes me warily.

"Catch? Uh-oh." I brace myself for him to explain we'll need to take back the Bentley or paint the car lime green or have me do the limbo in a bikini.

"He wants you to deliver it. Today. Now, in fact."

Raymond's hand comes out of his pocket, a key fob dangling.

"Me? *Now?*" My heart plummets. I should be relieved to have an excuse to be away from the show-room when Austin arrives, but suddenly I'm not. If I'm not here to talk about the car, he might leave and never return. When will I see him again?

Raymond jingles the fob. "We're not busy this morning. Lethbridge specifically wants you—says you're the one who finally convinced him, and he wants to thank you personally."

"Then why can't he come in and pick it up?" I demand.

Raymond shrugs. "Billionaires don't think like we do. He's dropping a lot of money on this car—cash—and delivery is one of our services. Please, Brooke."

I know Raymond's right—it's part of our job to offer

great customer service. If a rich client wants a car he's been waffling on for three months delivered to his house, we deliver it to his house.

"If I drive it over, how do I get back?" I know how—I can do a ride share, call a cab, hell, walk to a bus stop. But I'm irritated.

"Call me when you're there and I'll pick you up," Raymond offers. Generous of him, because he hates driving in Phoenix traffic. I find this ironic from a man who sells cars, but he likes them to stay pristine, and prefers to drive on the track.

"I'm expecting a client of my own," I say, trying not to sound desperate.

"I wouldn't ask, but Lethbridge is an important customer."

Raymond is being perfectly reasonable, and I'm not. Austin might or might not buy the Maserati while Simon's a sure sale, and he's acquiring a very expensive car. Raymond trusts me to get it there safely.

I snatch the key from Raymond's hand. "Most people have a car like this delivered in a transport to a secure garage."

"Lethbridge has a secure garage, but he doesn't want to see it coming off a truck. He'd rather watch it heading toward him on the street, driven by a real person. You. His words."

"Fine." I harden my voice. "Mike, when Mr. McLaughlin arrives, please go over the financials with him. Tell him I was detained."

"Mr. McLaughlin?" Mike gives me a puzzled look,

then his expression clears. "Oh, yeah. Austin. Got it. I'll sweet-talk him."

"Just tell him the numbers," I say in exasperation. "I'll be back as soon as I can."

"Take your time." Raymond frowns at me. "That car's not easily replaceable."

"I'll make sure it's in perfect condition once it slides from our insurance to his." I know Raymond is more worried about the car itself than the money—he loves them for their own sakes—but I don't know what I'm saying anymore.

I won't be here when Austin arrives, and that has me more upset than I care to acknowledge.

Austin

My brother Ryan drops me off at Brooke's showroom at 12:15. He's heading home for lunch and a little canoodling with Calandra—not that he admits the second part, but I know my oldest brother well.

Ryan knows me well in return. He's always been my champion, defending me against our middle two brothers, mostly Zach, when they looked for someone to pick on. As the youngest, I was a natural target.

Ryan halts his SUV smoothly in front of the dealership, casting a longing glance at the flashy cars visible through the windows. "Must be nice," he said. "But I have a little one to save for now." Ryan's proud expression tells me he's not really regretful. "Say hi to Brooke for me."

"Will do. If she even speaks to me."

"She will—to take your check if nothing else." Ryan sketches me a salute. "Good luck, bro."

"Thanks." I slide out of the SUV and lift my hand as he drives off.

I square my shoulders and walk toward the showroom. I'd spent about fifteen minutes in the bathroom at the office making sure my hair was combed but not so neat it appeared I spent fifteen minutes on it. A sudden gust of dry wind puffs around the corner and tangles it up again.

The wind carries dust, and my shirt, dark blue—Brooke likes blue—gets filmed with a sandstone-colored layer of it.

I yank open the showroom door and force myself to amble inside. I don't care what I look like, right? I've come to decide whether to buy a car. The fact that I took half an hour choosing what to wear today has nothing to do with Brooke and I sharing one hell of a burning kiss last night.

And what a kiss. The hard-on I've had off and on since that kiss threatens to return. It had taken a cold shower and a boring documentary on the nature of gravity to calm it down last night. I did finally sleep, but dreams of Brooke—her hair silken under my hands, her skin beneath my lips, the softening of her face as she relaxes to me—did not make my night easier.

But I'm fine now, right? Not a care in the world.

"Hey, Austin. Welcome back." Mike greets me. "Ice-water? Iced tea? Chilled wine?" I'm sure he's offering because he's seen the ramrod in my pants, but he continues, "It's a hot one today."

True. It's 110 F already, and only the noon hour. "No, I'm good. I'm here to let Brooke convince me to buy a Maserati I don't need."

"Brooke's not in." Mike's expression turns apologetic. "She had to deliver a car. I'll be walking you through the paperwork."

"Of course she did." I deflate like a popped balloon, which includes the pesky hard-on, which is now completely gone.

Mike can't be much younger than I am. He has a tan from whatever outdoor activities he likes—in our sunshine, walking to the mailbox will give you a tan— dark hair and brown eyes. He's in a crisp button-down shirt and tie, expensive suit pants, and polished black shoes. The epitome of a professional salesman, the kind of guy Brooke wants working for her.

"She really did have to deliver the car," Mike continues. "I was here when Raymond asked her to do it. Difficult client, wicked fine car. Limited edition Lamborghini."

"I get it." Pacifying a man who'd bought a car worth a couple million beat talking Austin into maybe purchasing a base model a twentieth that price. No contest as to who got special treatment.

"She's very sorry to have missed you."

I hold up my hand. "You don't have to apologize for

her. I'm guessing she ran as soon as she had the opportunity."

Mike looks puzzled. "Why would she?"

"Because she ..." I shake my head. "I'll tell you the truth—Brooke and I used to go out. It did not end well."

"Oh." Mike's mouth pulls down. "I thought that might be the case. I won't mention it again."

"Not your fault." I try to relax. "I'm still interested in the car. It has nothing to do with her. Or relationships. Or anything."

"Gotcha. Come on over to my desk, and I'll get things rolling. Sure you don't want wine?"

I'd over-imbibed last night, and it had gained me nothing. No headache—Brooke had been right about that—but my stomach ached. Nothing to do with the wine, though. The knot in it had tightened every time I thought about seeing Brooke today.

"No, I'm good. Thanks." I follow Mike to a desk on one side of the showroom. A black gull-winged Lamborghini rests five feet away, drawing my appreciative gaze.

If Brooke were nearby, I wouldn't even notice it.

"Here we go." Mike shoves two folders in front of me. "Lease terms and purchase terms." He touches each folder in turn. "I'll let you go over those, then you can ask me any questions."

I open folder one, which lays out the lease terms—down payment, months, interest rate, etc. Again I regret Brooke isn't here. I love to watch her run down the sales nitty-gritty, talking numbers in her smooth voice while her lithe fingers dance over the pages. She has the patter down. I melt listening to her. I'd buy slices of moldy cheese from Brooke when she's in that mode.

I finish the lease folder and turn to the purchase one. I prefer to purchase—I keep cars a long time. Good ones will last many years if they're taken care of.

My eyes widen as I scan the pages—different monthly payments depending on terms of the loan, but each choice is possible only with a whopping amount down.

I whistle. "This is a lot of clams."

"It's a lot of car," Mike says in sympathy.

"A car I have no business buying." I think of Ryan, who's saving every penny for my forthcoming niece or nephew, and of Zach and Ben, both being frugal for their new lives.

Mike's cheerful demeanor evaporates into concern. "Please don't walk away from the deal until you've talked to Brooke. She would *not* be happy with me."

"I'd tell her it's not your fault. Don't worry, I'm not saying no. Just ..."

I shake my head and close and stack the folders. Why can't I be a cool billionaire and casually drop a wad of cash on the desk and snap up the keys?

Because this is real life. I'm about to tell Mike I'll think about it and return when Brooke is around, when his cell phone rings.

"Speak of the devil," he says, as the name "Brooke Marsh" flashes on his screen. Mike answers. "What's up, boss?" Mike listens for a bit, then nods. "Sure thing. Be right there."

"Something wrong?" I ask as he hangs up.

"No," Mike says, unworried. "Brooke needs a ride back. Raymond was supposed to pick her up, but he's with another client. This guy, Simon. He's a smooth-talking Brit loaded with money, but he won't fork out for Brooke's cab fare. And I should *not* have told you that."

I'm on my feet. "I'll go." I don't at all like the idea of a smooth-talking, rich Englishman alone with Brooke. "What's the address?"

Mike has no problem giving it to me, and before he puts down his phone, I'm out the door.

Chapter Four

Brooke

SIMON LETHBRIDGE IS in his forties, with dark hair turning to salt-and-pepper, and a smooth British accent. A Hampshire accent, he'd told me—there is no single British or English accent, he said, as the cadence and word choice can vary from county to county, even within twenty miles.

Never having been to England, I have to take his word for it. Simon's pleased with the car and very grateful to me for delivering it personally.

"It's why I like your dealership," he says as we stand in his garage, looking over the Lamborghini. He's built a two-story garage that's larger than his house and has more security than a bank vault. "So many companies take your money and turn their backs. You are far more friendly."

Simon smiles as he speaks. He's always pleasant,

never going over the line to inappropriate. He simply likes to admire, tinker with, and drive great cars.

"It's a small local business," I say.

"And will be yours soon, I hear." Simon beams at me. "Well done."

"Thank you." I slide out my cell phone. "Well, I have to be getting back."

"Of course."

Simon is polite and friendly, even when he's driving a hard bargain. I call Raymond, who tells me he's with a client, and that I have to make other arrangements. I'm not surprised, and dial Mike.

Mike says he'll be here, and I hang up to find Simon lounging against his new car. "It's a pity to ride around in a monster like this by myself."

Is it? "I don't know." I drop my phone into my purse. "I sure enjoyed driving it over here."

Predictably, I'd gotten a lot of stares, including from two small boys who were overawed. I'd waved at them, and they'd waved frantically back, not stopping until their mom turned the corner and took them out of sight. I'd also been propositioned three times. *Sure you can handle that car, babe? Want me to handle you ... I mean it ... for you?*

I'd driven on without acknowledgement.

Simon is studying me, his brown eyes softening. "Perhaps you and I could go for a spin sometime?"

"Oh." Okay, proposition number four. Except Simon isn't leering or making suggestive comments. He's phrasing it so I can turn him down, no big deal.

I should say yes. Simon is good-looking, nice, filthy rich, and of course, owns great automobiles. It *would* be fun to drive around town with him or on the highways or back roads. He's single—divorced a long time ago—and is somewhat shy. He's not the type to hang out at a singles' bar or do online dating.

He's also smart, well-read, likes good food and wine, and isn't obnoxiously sexy. Or obnoxious in any way.

Why does Austin spring into my head with the word *obnoxious*? I should forget about him. Austin and Simon do have in common their appreciation of wine and cars, but there the comparison ends. Simon is classical music while Austin is the latest pop. Simon is fine china and silver, dressed up even when he wears casual clothes. He'd never share a disgusting hot dog with me on a paper plate on the bank of the Salt River after a day of tubing, and he'd never dance naked, belting out tunes and making me laugh until I nearly fall out of bed.

I don't need Austin and his antics. He and I are like oil and fire—not a good combination.

Simon would be cool water. Austin singes and burns. Simon would soothe.

He senses my hesitation. "It's all right. Just a suggestion." Simon's smile implies that I won't hurt his feelings if I say no.

"Oh, I ..."

Simon laughs, the sound quiet. "I said it's all right, Brooke. You're a beautiful woman. I have to try. Do me a favor. Think about it? Call me if you'd like. You know my number."

He's so nice, so unassuming, that I want to say yes just to make him feel better. But would that be fair to him? Or to me?

I have no idea. Maybe Simon's right that I should think about it.

I open my mouth to at least agree to giving it some thought, when a car rumbles down the street. It's a gray Mercedes C 300, the same one that sat in our locked lot all night and unnerved me when I spotted it this morning.

My heart bangs, my throat tightening. "Uh. I think that's my ride."

"Yes, it seems to be."

Simon straightens up and walks with me out the open doors of the garage. He signals the car in, probably figuring it's Mike behind the wheel.

Austin pulls into the driveway, stops the car, and steps out.

I feast my eyes on him. Simon, poor Simon, fades to almost nothing as the vibrant Austin moves toward us. His shirt, even dusty, brings out the blue of his eyes, and his hair is pleasantly rumpled.

Austin gives me a cordial nod and darts his gaze into Simon's garage, spying the new car inside. "Oh, very nice."

"Like it?" Simon indicates the Lamborghini. "This lady had to talk me into it, but I'm so very glad she did."

Simon sends me a fond glance, and Austin's eyes tighten. "She's trying to talk me into a Ghibli."

Simon makes an approving nod. "Those are nice. Move well. Take it out for a fast spin—really see what she can do."

"Good idea." Austin's gaze flicks to me, and I see he's applying the *she* in Simon's sentence to me.

Typical. I really should blow off Austin and take Simon up on his offer. Then Austin smiles, and I know Simon doesn't stand a chance.

Austin shifts his attention to the other cars in Simon's collection. "Is that a Lotus?"

"Indeed, it is. Come in, I'll show you. We haven't met ... I'm Simon Lethbridge." He holds out his hand.

"Austin McLaughlin." Austin and Simon share a handshake.

"McLaughlin. There's a McLaughlin Renovations around here—I see their signs in my neighbor's yards."

"That's us. I'm a junior member. We work on many houses in this area. Bring them up to code without violating the restrictions on changing a historic property."

Simon lives in Encanto, an older patch of town with some houses dating back a hundred years and more. There are mansions in the neighborhood, but also many smaller homes, like Simon's. I'm not surprised the McLaughlins' services are used a lot.

"How about a bottle of wine?" Simon says as he strolls into his garage. "To celebrate my new car. What do you like, Austin?" He peers at Austin as though testing him.

"Can't go wrong with a good pinot noir. Best grapes ever."

"Excellent." Simon's tone means Austin has passed his test. "Brooke? That all right with you? I also have a Riesling, chilled—good on a hot day."

"I shouldn't drink at all. Have to work."

"Americans." Simon shakes his head. "One glass of wine on your lunch hour won't hurt you. You'll not be downing the bottle."

"Thank you, but I really have to be getting back," I say hastily.

"Nonsense. A glass to toast a completed sale. I'll just pop down to the cellar."

Austin's eyes widen. "You have a *wine cellar*?"

"I had it put in. It's not much, only a space under the house, large enough to keep a decent stock on hand. I don't collect—I just drink the stuff." Shrugging, Simon slips out the back door of the garage, leaving it ajar. The garage is air-conditioned, but hot wind snakes through the open front doors.

Austin watches Simon go in admiration. He turns to me, lips parted to continue the conversation, but I cut him off.

"What are you doing here?"

Austin doesn't lose his grin. "Oh, nice. I drive all the way down here, and that's how you greet me?"

"I'm serious. I remember calling Mike, and Mike saying he'd be right over."

"Mike is trying to make a living. I'm on my lunch hour. What happens if Mike loses a big commission because he's running an errand for you? If *I'm* late back, my mom snarls at me, but I stay an hour after, and she's sweet again."

I wave my hands in exasperation. "Never mind. You're just trying to mess with me again."

"Maybe. Plus I promised Mike I'd talk to you before I turned down the Ghibli."

I stop. "Wait. What? You don't want it?"

"Still thinking about it. It's a lot of money to part with. That the best you can do? What about a friends and family discount?"

"That *is* the friends and family discount." Why am I having a hard time breathing? Oh, yeah. Austin makes me crazy.

"Aw." His voice goes soft. "You're saying we're friends. I like that."

His words evaporate my anger, and suddenly, I'm melting. Again. Damn it—how does he do this to me?

"Here we are." Simon wafts back inside with a bottle in one hand, three long-stemmed glasses in the other. "Have a corkscrew somewhere. Ah."

He sets the glasses on a trolley of tools, reaches into his pocket, and pulls out a corkscrew. Expertly, he removes the cork, pours a splash into a glass, and holds it out to Austin.

Austin takes in the scent of the wine. "Nice nose. Great body too."

Does he glance at me when he says *great body*, or am I imagining that?

Austin sips. His smart-ass look falls away and he gazes at the wine in true appreciation. "That is one superb vintage."

"I bought a case last time I was in France. Well, let's drink up."

Simon fills each glass to the brim. I decide I'll take a few polite sips, but the wine truly is remarkable. Most wines I drink are good—because why drink a bad wine? —but this one is extraordinary. I can taste the wind and sunshine, the sweetness of the grape, and the bite of the wood of its barrel. *Terroir*—the environment in which the wine is produced is called. Simon must have spent a wad on this bottle, let alone the case.

Austin is effusive in his praise. "It's like sunshine in a glass."

"Yes, it is rather nice, isn't it?" Simon uses his typical understatement.

"Thank you for letting me partake. It's an honor." Austin and Simon shake hands again. I barely stop myself telling them to get a room.

I drink the entire glass, not wanting to let such a wonderful liquid go to waste. Austin drains his too but to my surprise refuses a refill.

"I do need to return Brooke to her job," he tells Simon. "We working people can't drink wine all afternoon, much as we'd like to."

"I understand." Simon pours himself another

without apology. "Thank you again, Brooke. It was very nice of you to come out of your way to placate me."

"Not at all," I manage. Austin is watching me, assessing.

"First-class service. I shall give your business five stars on whatever that app is called."

"Not necessary." My words emerge breathlessly. "Thank you so much for the wine."

"Oh ... tell you what. Take a bottle with you."

"No." I hold up my hands. "I can't. Thanks, though."

"Don't be silly. Wait a tick." Simon's out the door.

"I really can't accept it," I tell Austin, a waver in my voice. "Raymond has a policy. He doesn't want anyone accusing us of cutting a price because of an expensive gift."

"No problem." Austin crosses to the back door, peering out as though trying to see how Simon gets to his wine cellar. "He can give it to me. I don't work for Raymond."

"I—" I snap my mouth shut. Why am I arguing? What does it matter? Except, as I say, Austin makes me crazy.

"One bottle of pinot noir," Simon sings out as he enters the garage—Austin had retreated from the door. "A beautiful wine for a beautiful woman."

He hands the bottle to me. Austin, the shit, stands back, arms folded, and I have to take it.

"Thank you. I really can't—"

"I do hate that word. *Can't.*" Simon turns to Austin. "Tell her to enjoy it."

"I will. Thank you, Simon." Yet another handshake. Austin peers wistfully at the Lamborghini then resolutely moves from it. "Great to meet you. Ready, Brooke?"

I clutch the bottle while I shake Simon's hand. Simon pulls me close and kisses my cheek.

Austin's eyes narrow at that, and his lips flatten, but he says nothing. He takes my arm to steer me from the garage, his fingers strong.

Austin opens his car door for me. I tuck the wine into the back seat, covering it with a towel to keep it from the sun. Austin waits until I'm settled before he closes the door and retreats to the driver's side of the car. He starts up, waves to Simon, who waves cheerily back, and Austin drives off.

"Good thing he kept that kiss to your cheek." Austin's voice is a growl, his good humor gone. "I'd have decked him. Wine or no wine."

"He didn't mean anything by it." I'm fairly certain. "Excited about the Lamborghini, loosened up with wine."

"Huh." Austin glances at me. "I know the look a man has when he wants to get into a girl's pants. I saw it on Simon's face."

"Into a girl's pants? Are we teenagers?"

"No matter what you call it, he wants it."

"You're dreaming."

"Nope." Austin relaxes as he turns onto Thomas

and heads for Seventh Avenue. "I can see why you'd fall for him though. A garage full of fantastic cars, a wine cellar, with that laidback British thing going for him. Hell, *I'd* date him."

Austin pretends to be offhand, but I hear the tension in his voice.

"There is nothing between me and Simon Lethbridge," I say stiffly.

Austin shoots me another glance. I can't tell whether he believes me or not, but he says nothing.

After a few blocks of silence, I venture, "Do you really not want the Ghibli?"

"Not a question of wanting, love. It's not like I'm a guy with a wine cellar and a garage full of luxury cars who can buy anything on a whim."

"You don't need to be. You're fine the way you are."

Austin turns his head to pin me with a stare before snapping his attention back to the road. His shoulders tighten and he grips the wheel.

I hadn't said the words to placate him or be condescending. Austin truly is fine the way he is. He's not fake. When I'm with Austin, I know I'm beside the real person inside. He doesn't put on a persona or a show. He really is the goof who dances naked in his bedroom, belting out a tune and shaking his ass.

I smile at the memory. Austin darts his gaze to me and frowns. "What's so funny?"

"Nothing. You don't have to decide on the car today—and you don't have to buy *that* car. Take all the time you need. We can order whatever you want."

"Yeah?" He leans back in his seat. "That does help. Thanks."

"We're known for our customer service."

I say it in my businesslike voice, but Austin's lips twitch. "I am not going to touch that." He's quiet for another stoplight then says casually, "That's a great bottle of wine. Made for sharing. Want to?"

" ..." I meant for a sound to come out of my mouth, but only a squeak emerges.

"Is that a yes?"

"I have to work," I blurt. "You keep the wine. I told you I can't accept it."

"I mean after work. We can take it to your house, or mine. Just to talk, I promise, and enjoy the pinot, like it should be enjoyed. Like we did last night."

Last night—sure. The talking had been fun. I'd let myself be at ease with him. Then I'd kissed him. My lips still tingled from it.

"I ... uh."

"Forget it." Austin's brows slam together. "I thought maybe we could be friends again, but I guess we can't."

He turns the corner onto Camelback, and not long later, he's circling the block to reach the back door of the dealership.

My heart is pounding when I step out of his car, my chest aching. I want to be friends with him too—Austin and I had wonderful times together. But I know he's right. The minute we try, our instincts will want to take things further, and we'd end up hurting. Like I am now.

I expect Austin to tear off back through the gates as soon as I'm out, but he parks and climbs from the car.

"I'd like to look at the Maserati one more time," he says to my stunned face.

"Sure. I'll just ... um ... keys ..."

"I'll wait."

I scuttle toward the showroom, fumbling with my purse and tottering on my heels. Sweat from the merciless sun runs down my face, ruining all the makeup I'd carefully applied.

What is happening to me? I'm always dignified, poised, together—until I'm around Austin. He is so, so bad for me.

I feel him behind me, and I turn. He's leaning on his car, arms folded, sunglasses fixed on me. The heat doesn't bother him at all—he's cool and calm, like I should be.

But I never will be calm as long as Austin is watching me, and still feel his hot kisses on my lips.

———

Austin

"Austin! That really you? Great to see you."

A large man emerges into the lot from the showroom after he holds the door for Brooke. He stops her, hugs her, and kisses her cheek, but this doesn't bug me the way it had when Simon had done the same thing.

The man is Cedric Marsh, Brooke's older brother.

As Brooke rushes inside, Cedric strides toward me, his warm laugh as big as the rest of him. Cedric claims to be all thumbs when it comes to sports, but if I managed a football team, I'd sign him to simply stand there and intimidate the opposing side.

Cedric catches me in a bear hug. I can't breathe, but I'm glad to see him. I thump his back, and he lets me loose.

"How the hell are you?" he booms. "I was in the area and thought, why not stop by and say hey to my baby sister? And here you are. You two together again?"

His brown eyes are hopeful, but I have to disappoint him. "Nope. I'm buying a car. Well, maybe buying it. *If* I sell everything I own and all my blood and a few organs."

"Ha. Yeah, they're pricey. It's an investment, though, and not just something you drive to work."

That's true. Like a rare wine meant for display instead of drinking, or great artwork.

"I'm also trying to convince Brooke to share a bottle of wine with me," I hear myself say. "Can you give me any help?"

"I'd love to, but I'd like my skin to stay on the outside of my body." Cedric shakes his head. "She is one stubborn woman, my sister. I hope you convince her. She was better when she was with you. Know what I mean?"

I'm touched he thinks so, and I wonder if it's true. "Except for all the arguing," I say wryly.

"Even with all the arguing." Cedric gives me an

appraising glance. "Maybe because of it. She needs to get out of her shell more."

We both turn to watch Brooke walk out of the showroom, key in hand. She's cool and composed in her beige sheath dress, with a length of blue beads around her neck and matching earrings to give the outfit a shot of color. Her high-heeled sandals are blue as well.

She does tend to retreat behind her businesslike demeanor, but that shell is mighty nice to look at.

"Do you want another test drive?" Brooke asks me in a hard voice.

Another line she's feeding me that I'm not going to touch. Not with big brother Cedric next to me. Cedric and I are friends, and he wants Brooke and me back together, but if I upset his baby sister, I will be the loser.

"Oh hey, tell you what," Cedric interrupts before I can answer. "My folks are having a big supper on Saturday night. A cookout and pool party. Why don't you come, Austin? They'd love to see you."

Brooke's face squeezes like someone kicked her. Cedric doesn't seem to notice, all smiles.

I contrast him to the man I'd just met—Simon. Simon is quiet and slender, seemingly shy, but I sensed in his understated way that he'd been anxious to impress both me and Brooke.

Cedric simply wants everyone to be happy.

I grin at him and then Brooke. "Sounds great," I say with enthusiasm. "Tell them I'll be there."

Chapter Five

Brooke

I INVENT all kinds of excuses to avoid my family's party at the end of the week, but nothing works. Mom and Dad want me there, according to Cedric's texts.

It's Dad's one text—*Looking forward to seeing you, Punkin,* that clinches my decision. I've been too busy to visit for a while, and usually Dad never says a word. I know he likes the whole family together, and he is fond of Austin.

I sigh and try to figure out what to wear. I don't know why this matters for a family cookout, but I choose and discard one outfit after the other.

I wonder if Austin will show up. He and Cedric, who'd been good friends before Austin and I broke up, had decided it was a great idea. Neither of them asked for my opinion. But why should they? Why should

Austin's weekend activities have anything to do with me?

Austin hadn't taken another test drive in the Ghibli after all. He'd looked over the car and asked our mechanic to show him the engine. While the two of them, with Cedric as a rapt audience, had talked about specs, I'd retreated to the coolness of the showroom.

Austin had returned the key to Mike, only waving at me when he left. He'd kept the wine, which was fine with me.

Why had I felt so bereft when he'd walked away? It wasn't like I still had feelings for him, right?

We had argued a lot when we were together, going at it heatedly. It was better that we'd broken up. I told myself that often.

Austin was impetuous, whimsical, didn't take things seriously. I'd been struggling to make my way in the world, to prove I could be more than tits-and-ass in a job Austin had encouraged me to try.

I'd been touchy about it, I know. Every day was a struggle—every day I was more or less told I didn't belong. I thought that if I worked hard enough, I'd show my worth, and people would cease judging me by my outside and accept me for my inside—at least the people I worked with and for. I'd accomplished that, more or less, but it had been a fight.

Austin had been very supportive, but he'd gone over the top, threatening to have a serious talking to with anyone who treated me without respect. I'd tried to point out I had to stand on my own, without my boyfriend glowering behind me. Austin didn't quite grasp that, which had led to some big blowouts.

And yet, whenever we'd made things up, it had been wonderful. Even while we'd argued, something in me had burned with excitement. We boiled over when we fought, and scorched the sheets when we came back together.

The constant ups and downs in our relationship, though, had wearied me, especially when I had to stand strong every day at my job. I couldn't face fights with Austin after work when I'd been so stressed during my shifts, and he refused to take anything except protecting me seriously. It was frustrating.

The final straw came was the day he'd arrived to pick me up from work, and I'd been visibly upset. Two of the sales guys had jumped all over my case that day, saying I'd stolen clients from them. I hadn't—clients I'd originally talked to had returned and asked for me, though the understanding had been that I'd turn them over to the sales guys who were senior to me when they were ready to purchase. But the clients stated they'd only deal with me, and Raymond had backed me up. The sales guys had talked about never trusting me and never working with me again—they'd said worse things about me when they thought I couldn't hear them.

When I'd emerged from the showroom that night, Austin had demanded to know why I was unhappy. I'd foolishly told him. Austin parked his car, stormed inside, and had it out with the two sales guys—thankfully no customers had been there.

Austin had yelled at them and commanded them to show me respect or answer to him. The two sales guys, after a lively argument with Austin, had quit on the spot, and had even threatened to sue Raymond. Raymond hadn't been happy and had come close to firing me. I'd been so angry and humiliated that Austin and I had gone home to have the mother of all fights.

I'd told him he had no business being my guard dog, and that I had to stand on my own or I'd never make it. Austin had told me I was ungrateful and too proud to accept help. Things had escalated from there.

I could have lost my job for his posturing, and I told him so. The sales guys could try to sue him for assault, though Austin hadn't touched them. But they might go after him for threatening them. The other sales staff would be furious with me for causing trouble.

I told him he didn't understand that I had to live my own life, no matter how hard it was, and he needed to back off. Austin, shouting in return, said he didn't like me dictating how to run our relationship.

We'd screamed at each other until we were hoarse, only this time, there was no hot sex afterward as we cooled down.

Austin told me that when I was ready to talk reasonably to call him. I told *him* that when he calmed down and understood what an asshole he was being, to call *me*.

He'd stormed out, and never came back.

I'd waited for my phone to ring. It hadn't. No calls, no texts. I'd start to pick up my phone to call him, and then get mad all over again. If he wanted this relationship to work, he'd reach out. Right?

Our silence had stretched a week, then a month, then a year. I kept expecting Austin to get in touch. When he didn't, I feared to call him, not wanting his drawling voice to tell me to go away, we were done.

We hung in limbo for a while, then I'd heard he'd moved on with his life, partying, hanging out with other women. I don't know if he slept with these women, and I don't want to know.

So I moved on too. I dated a few guys, but none of them compared to Austin, and I gave up.

For some reason, I still checked my phone every day to see if there was any word from Austin. For a year and a half, there never was.

Now I'm about to own the dealership I struggled to survive in, Austin and I have hung out at a wine bar, and he's coming to my family's cookout.

The sloppy shorts and T-shirt I planned to wear fly into the corner. A nicer buttoned shirt, crisp cargo shorts, and a pair of gold sandals come out instead. Plus gold earrings, rings on my fingers, and a bracelet. I won't be able to swim, because my hair will tangle like shit if I do. I comb it and braid it back, as though I'm anticipating a laidback day with family.

Laidback, sure. I went to a salon last night for a trim and a mani-pedi for *me*—I don't care how Austin thinks I look.

I'm not nervous *at all* as I pull into my parents' house in north Scottsdale. At all.

My folks live not far over the Phoenix-Scottsdale border, in a large mid-century house. They have a huge yard with a wide swimming pool, tall ironwood trees, and a flower and herb garden my mother nurses throughout the year.

I scan the yard and back patio for Austin, but he's nowhere in sight. I'm relieved ... and disappointed. Relieved alone should be the correct reaction, but I'm never sensible when it comes to Austin.

"You look so pretty, honey." My mother, several inches shorter than I am, pulls me into one of her squishy hugs. She releases me to observe me critically. "But also tired. You been getting enough sleep?"

"Yes." *No.* I've been dreaming of Austin, or else lying awake reliving our kiss, plus thinking about the sound of his voice, the touch of his hand, the scent of his skin ... Hence, continued bags under my eyes.

"Oh, there's Cedric." Mom hoists her hand to greet my brother.

I spin around, sure Austin will be with him, and deflate when I see Cedric alone. I love my brother, so I should be ecstatic to see him. Not drooping in despondency.

"Hey Mom." Cedric bends nearly double to embrace her. He takes after my dad, who is also a giant. "Sis." Cedric crushes me in one of his large hugs. "How's my Babbling Brooke?"

He's called me that since I'd learned to talk and would go on about nothing, making up my own words.

"Fine," I say when he lets me go. "What about you?"

"Oh, you know." Cedric shrugs. "Working, eating, sleeping. You only saw me Monday, so not much has changed. Heard from Austin?"

I jump. "No. Why should I? He's friends with you."

"Okay, okay, calm down." Cedric takes a step back. "Just asking."

"Austin called *me*," Mom breaks in. "Making sure it was okay if he crashed our little party. The sweetheart. It'll be nice to see him."

"If he comes," I mutter.

"He will," Cedric says with confidence.

Mom, who shares my brown eyes and black hair, hers now with a touch of gray, studies me shrewdly. "Do you want him to, or not?"

"It doesn't matter to me." I feign indifference, but my stomach twists. "Like I said, he's Cedric's friend. I'm not getting in the way of that."

"Good for you, honey." Mom pats my arm, and the pat becomes a fond rub. "We can all be friends."

I can't manage a reply. Mom takes pity on me and moves the conversation to other things.

Mom has invited some old friends and neighborhood ones, who arrive bearing food. I haven't seen many of them for a while, so I'm constantly hugging or answering questions about how I've been.

While I'm performing this flurry of greeting, I see

Austin stroll through the open gate next to the driveway and into the backyard.

He's in shorts and a polo top, which show off his muscular arms and legs. Track shoes complete his outfit, like he'll go running when he's done here. He has a pack slung over one shoulder—maybe he's brought his swimming gear. That means he'll be in a small bathing suit, nothing else, as he dives gracefully into the water ...

I completely forget what I'm about to say to one of my mom's friends, and the woman gives me a puzzled look. Her expression clears when she sees me staring at Austin, adding to my embarrassment. Everyone knows about us.

Austin isn't trying to find me. He greets Cedric, the two of them clasping hands and thumping backs. Then Austin makes for my parents, who are holding court near the pool. Evening has fallen, and misters cool the air.

I start for them even as Austin greets my mom, she pulling him down to her for a hug.

"Austin," Mom says. "We've missed you."

"Good to see you again, son," my dad agrees in his booming voice.

"You too," Austin says. "I should have called more often, but ..."

"We understand." Mom really does understand, which is a little disconcerting. She knows all about the breakup. "Oh, what's this?"

Austin has unslung the shoulder bag and removes a

bottle of wine. "For you," he says, presenting it to my mom with a flourish.

I'm near enough to see that it's the bottle from Simon I told him to keep. Austin obviously hasn't opened it, or drunk it, or shared it with another woman. He hands it to my mom with a smile, and she gazes at the bottle in delight.

"You shouldn't have," Mom gushes. "No, really. This is a lovely gift."

Mom knows a thing or two about wine. She's the one who taught me.

"Glad you like it. Do me a favor." Austin slides his arm around Mom's waist. "Don't save it for a special occasion. Drink it now and enjoy it."

"You are so right. Thank you, Austin." She kisses his cheek. "Isn't this a nice gift, Brooke?"

Mom carefully holds up the pinot noir. Austin catches my eye and dares me to say anything.

"It is," Brooke said. "A good wine. Very thoughtful."

Austin's eyes flicker, but he lets it go. "It is good to see you again, Viola. Now." He rubs his hands together. "Where's your awesome food? I'm starving."

Mom laughs. "Brooke, take Austin in and show him where he can fill his plate."

"Sure thing." I woodenly thrust my hand through the crook of Austin's arm and pull him toward the house.

"It's not cheesy giving your mom that wine," Austin says as we step into the coolness of the house.

"You had no interest in it, and I hated to see it go to waste. She and your dad will appreciate it like it's meant to be."

"It was your bottle. You could do with it what you want." I try to keep my tone cool, but he's not fooled.

"Your brother invited me, remember?" Austin says. "I did not come here to make you uncomfortable."

"Who says you're making me uncomfortable?" I bathe Austin in a smile and lead him through the kitchen to the large dining room. Two entrances feed into this room, one from the kitchen and one from the living room. Food covers the table, with a stack of plates on the end, buffet style. We're to eat wherever we can find a place.

"Your entire body tells me I am." Austin takes up a plate, but he's looking at me, not the food. Fortunately no one else is in the dining room at the moment.

"Someone is full of himself. Why *did* you decide to come tonight? You could have met with Cedric and my parents another time. You know everyone out there is busy assuming we're back together."

Austin shrugs. "Well, you know me. I always accept a challenge. Never say never."

My heart skips a beat. That had been our catch phrase throughout our relationship, what we'd say when daring ourselves to take things farther, deeper.

"A challenge, was it?" I say, pretending his words don't affect me. "Sure you didn't come to prove something?"

"Huh." Austin's mouth is hard, his playfulness fleeing. "You talk about egos, but the biggest one in this room is yours."

That stings. "What are you attacking me for? I didn't invite you—Cedric did. I don't give a shit if you gave my parents Simon's wine. They'll appreciate it."

"More than you did."

I had been reaching for a plate, but I snatch my hand back. "Seriously? How have I pissed you off now? By trying to talk you into buying a car?"

Austin plops a blob of potato salad—my mom's with new potatoes, olive oil, and roasted garlic—onto his plate. "This has nothing to do with the damned car. It's about you, and how you push me away when you don't like how things are going."

"I'm not pushing you away. I haven't even talked to you for nearly two years. Not that you bothered trying to get in touch."

"No?" Austin drops a piece of roasted chicken next to the potato salad. "I remember telling you that any time you were ready, you could call me. You never did, did you?"

"I remember saying the same thing to you. Hmm, no calls. Anyway, you didn't wait very long before you were out with other people."

"A year." His fork hovers above the chicken. "I waited a year, Brooke. What was I supposed to do? Pine away at home? And excuse me, you went out with other guys. Our friends made sure to tell me about every single one."

"Only after they told me you were hanging out at clubs, with women all over you."

"Well, I didn't notice you becoming a nun."

My hands ball, my pounding pulse giving me a headache. "I do not have to take this." Saying it out loud gives me courage. I turn on my sandaled heel and stalk toward the door to the living room.

I hear Austin slam down his plate. In two seconds, he's in front of me, blocking my way out. He doesn't touch me—Austin only ever touches me in passion or friendliness.

"Running away? It's what you do, isn't it? Why don't you have the balls to stick it out?"

I tilt my head to meet his gaze. "Last time I checked, women don't have balls. If you're talking about guts, I have plenty of those. My gut is now telling me to walk away from you and don't let you intimidate me."

"Intimidate?" Austin's eyes widen. I've always loved his eyes. "Me? I'm the least intimidating person on the planet."

"That's what you think." It was true Austin never bullied, never browbeat, at least not with me. He smiled, coerced, coaxed, and melted me.

I try to move around him, but he sidesteps. "You know what? If you want to run, okay, run. I'll come with you."

I plant my hands on my hips. "How does that help me?"

"It doesn't. But we need to have this out. I'm not

going back outside to smile and laugh and pretend I'm ecstatic when there's all this shit simmering between us."

"And now we're back to you being full of yourself."

"Simmering." Austin runs his hand up and down the air that separates us. "We never truly finished our last fight, and it's burning us. If you have the guts you claim you do, come with me now, and let's finish this."

"Why?" I demand. "For closure?"

"Yes."

He's a solid wall in front of me. I could go back out through the kitchen, but my blood is hot, and I secretly agree with him. We need to clear the air.

Not only that, the idea of facing off with Austin, letting everything out, appeals to me. Arguing with him could be bracing.

"Fine," I say. "We'll go to my house. You drive."

His brows draw down. "Not exactly neutral ground."

"No, but if I throw you out, you'll have the means to get yourself home."

I don't trust myself going to his house or his office. Not because I think Austin is enough of a jerk to try to confine me in either place, but because I might capitulate once I'm on his territory.

I love his house, which he and his brothers restored, and his office—the McLaughlin family business—which radiates comfort and camaraderie. I might fling myself into Austin's arms if he takes me to his home. I'd nearly done so last Sunday night.

My house is crap, but it has four walls and a roof, and nothing sentimental associated with it. Easy for me to face him there.

Austin watches me for a long moment, then he gives me a stiff nod. "Fine. Your place. I drive."

He turns and strides out, trusting that I'll follow. I can easily run the other direction, back to the yard and my family and all their cronies, but I join him, and we leave the house together.

Chapter Six

Austin

BROOKE IS silent during the drive. She lives a few miles from her parents, in an uninspired Phoenix development, the kind that sprang up like mushrooms at the end of the last century. The development has faded now, the houses not that well-built to begin with, and now they're showing a lot of wear.

I pull into Brooke's driveway. Her home is small, with gravel in the tiny front yard and a palo verde tree to lend shade in the hot summer months.

A few solar lights line her driveway and front walk, pinpricks in the darkness. I hear kids screaming like banshees next door, and loud splashes as they slide into a backyard pool.

Brooke unlocks her front door. She walks firmly away from me after we enter, leaving me to close the door. I don't slam it, but all the walls shake.

"Damn." I study the crack in the plaster above the doorframe. "I don't remember it being this bad."

"It's a place to sleep. I don't need a lot."

She's always said that. Brooke can afford so much more than this, but she wants to show she's all about business success and not material pleasures. I'm far more into comfort, which was another thing we yelled about. She saw me as frivolous while I tried to show her a person can do well at their job and enjoy life too.

Brooke is behind the breakfast bar that separates the galley kitchen from the living room. She takes wine glasses down from a cupboard.

"What'cha doing?" I ask. The fevered heat that had swept me when we'd argued in her family's dining room has cooled, but we're both tense. "I thought we were going to fight."

"Doesn't mean we can't have a glass of wine and be civilized."

"Yeah? Does a break-up argument almost two years after the fact call for red or white?"

"How about a tawny port?"

"Interesting choice." I move to the breakfast bar and lean on it, resting my arms on its pristine surface. "I usually drink it with dessert."

"It's all I have." Brooke wrenches out the cork and trickles the red liquid into two narrow glasses.

I take the glass she shoves at me and raise it to her. "To ...whatever this is."

"Closure." Brooke touches her glass to mine and drinks.

I take a sip, and everything slows. This port might be all she has in the house, but Brooke knows how to choose a wine. It's full-bodied and sweet, but at the same time, not heavy. "Very nice."

"I don't have any cigars, sorry."

I give her a tight smile. "I'll forgive you." I don't smoke the things anyway, but she thinks I'm all about decadence.

Brooke takes another sip and sets the glass on the counter. "Are we going to do this?"

I don't want to. Airing our grievances now seems like a bad idea. I scrutinize her rundown kitchen cabinets, the small window through which I can clearly hear her neighbor's kids, and the out-of-date appliances.

"You know, your ex happens to be in the renovation business. We could do your house. We'd give you a true friends and family discount."

Brooke shrugs. "I spend all my time at work. Did you bring me here to drum up business for your brothers?"

"Not my job. That's Ryan and my dad."

Brooke's eyes narrow. "Yes, but you're sales and PR."

"True." I grin. "I'm the sweet-talker. Abby and I do that together now. She's overhauled the website and finds advertising opportunities, and I talk up the business to the ad platforms and make sure the ads bring in a decent return."

"I remember seeing your picture plastered on the

side of a bus last year," Brooke's lips twitch, amusement at my expense. "Didn't exactly help get you off my mind."

"Yeah, well." My face heats. "A PR firm's idea. We didn't renew our contract with them. But hey, it did bring in some business. People remembered it."

"It was … memorable." Her look turns teasing. "Sexy smile for the ladies."

"You know I was smiling at you, sweetheart." I point one finger around my glass at her.

Her frown returns. "Don't give me that."

"It's true. You are the one lady I can't get off my mind. So, here we go. You never called me, and I never called you. I figured if I did you'd lecture me on being hotheaded and rash, and we'd never solve anything. Then I started wanting you to call—I'd talk to you no matter what, but I guess you were too busy. After a while, I figured you weren't giving me time to cool off, you were dumping me."

"I wasn't dumping you." Brooke folds her arms. "Whenever we were together it was … stormy. Not always in a bad way, but it was hard to take. How could I think it would ever be different?"

"I get that. Or I'm trying to. You wanted to put all your focus on your job, to prove you were good at it. You sure proved it—you're about to own the business. You won. But the truth is, you never got in touch even when your battles were done. I took that to mean you no longer wanted to be with me. I can deal with that but wish you'd had the courtesy to *tell* me."

"Do *not* put this all on me." Her chin is up, Brooke's signal that she's full of righteous indignation. "If you were pouting and waiting for me to apologize, what was I supposed to do? Listen to you tell me how right you were?" She deflates a little. "By the time I was ready to swallow my pride and talk to you no matter what, hoping we could still be friends, Calandra's telling me you have a new girlfriend. Which you didn't have the courtesy to tell *me* about."

"Because I didn't think you'd care." My voice goes up in volume. "I wouldn't have even known you were alive without Cedric or your mom."

"Whose fault is that? From what they told me, you were pretty pissed off at me. I couldn't deal with soothing you down *and* concentrating on my job."

I shove from the counter and stride to the center of the living room. "Of course I was mad at you. I didn't think I was so high maintenance that you couldn't have a job *and* me at the same time."

"I never thought you were high maintenance. But look at us right now. *This* is what I'm talking about. I couldn't handle this plus the guys at the dealership expecting me to be a bubble-headed bimbo."

"And when I tried to help with that, you threw me out. Okay, I went a little far—I admit that, and I'm sorry. But you weren't mad that I told them they were dickheads—which they were—you were mad at me for embarrassing you."

Brooke charges around the counter to me, her wine forgotten. "Exactly. You assumed the weak little woman needed her macho boyfriend to stand up for her. I told you, I had to battle it out for myself."

"And you did it. I was only trying to make things a little easier for you. So at the end of the day you could *relax*. Which you seem incapable of doing."

"I don't *want* easy. I want to earn respect, show I'm not Babbling Brooke who will never be anything but cute and sassy."

She *was* cute and sassy, but I didn't dare say that right now. I'd be out the door, maybe with the bottle of port thrown at me.

"You seriously need to realize that people having your back doesn't mean you're weak," I shout. "It means they care about you."

"I'm not saying I was totally right." Brooke's volume increases to join mine. "I was scared and distracted, and you kept trying to fix everything for me, to cushion me when I wanted to face the world."

"Yeah? So sue me."

Brooke comes closer, but her hands are fists, nothing tender in her. "Then once I realized how much I missed you ... you were with someone else."

"Not really my fault." I know I'm not totally in the right here—my actions could have led to worse consequences than making a couple of guys so angry they quit the dealership. I'd lost my temper and wanted to defend my woman. I'd seen nothing wrong with that, but yes, I'd rushed in without thinking and could have lost her the job. But hell, I couldn't stand the look on Brooke's face when she'd left work that night—it had broken my heart. I'd had to do *something*. I thought she'd overreacted, but then, so had I.

"I wanted you to see I had options," I continue. "You showed me you had them too."

"And I hated every minute of it." Brooke is yelling now, leaning into me. "I didn't want those guys, and I never went out with any of them more than once. I wanted *you*, damn it. I realized I'd lost you, when you were the very person I needed most in my life." Her voice breaks on the last words.

I've wound myself up to yell back at her, but her speech floors me. I blink a few times, take another breath, let it out.

Tears glisten in the corners of her eyes. My Brooke, my strong lady who lets no one cow her, is crying.

I glimpse in her the same loneliness that's inside of me.

I close the small distance between us. Brooke doesn't step away, and I drag her against me. My hands go under her hair in its sleek, beautiful braid, and I pull her up for a passionate kiss.

Brooke stiffens, and I expect her to shove me away, but then she relaxes.

I taste her desire, her longing. Her hair warms my hands, her lips caress mine. The kiss turns deep, and I relearn the exact shape of her mouth, the sensation of her tongue.

Brooke closes her fingers around my shirt. She rises on her tiptoes, one arm going around me. I remember that too, how she'd hold me so close, as though she'd stay against me forever.

I can't get enough of her. I kiss and kiss her. If we don't stop, our mouths will be raw, but I don't care.

Eventually, Brooke breaks the kiss to catch her breath, but she doesn't move from me. "Austin ..."

I cup her face. "I've missed you. Damn, I've missed you."

"I've missed you too." Her voice is low, like silk to my jangled senses. "Can we ..."

"Shh." I kiss her lips. "Don't talk. We always screw up when we talk."

Brooke proves how wonderful she is by kissing me again. The room goes quiet. Even the kids next door have ceased their screaming—probably their parents have called them in for supper. The only sound is the hum of the air-conditioner clicking on and rattling above us, another thing she needs to replace.

Brooke runs her hands down my back, hooking her thumbs through my belt as she likes to. That way she can caress the hollow at the bottom of my spine, a place that spreads tingling fire through my body.

I rest my palms on her waist, and as our mouths work, I slide one hand up to cup her breast.

Brooke stills. I ease from the kiss but don't release her. Will she say no, tell me to get the hell out? Leave me hard and wanting, facing my empty house?

She regards me a long moment, while the breeze from the AC chills my skin and ruffles tendrils of her hair.

Then Brooke makes a raw sound in her throat, grabs my shirt, and shoves it upward, as though trying to tear it from my body.

I throw it off for her. Brooke gives me a savage smile and flattens her fingers to my chest, finding my nipples and making them tight. I'm burning now, my hard-on pushing against my zipper.

When Brooke leans in and licks the nipple, I can't stop my groan. "Oh, *man*, I've missed you."

"You mean the sex." Her whisper brushes her hot breath on my chest. She follows that by suckling me.

"Shit." I close my eyes and pull her closer. "I mean *you*. All of you. You are a hot, sexy woman, and it was hell staying away from you."

I don't want to restart the tirade about why each of us didn't call the other, so I shut up. Brooke suckles me until I'm crazy, and she's only doing it to my chest. Whoever thinks a man's nipples aren't sensitive is an idiot.

She lifts her head and wraps herself around me for another kiss. I let my roving fingers find the buttons that hold her shirt closed in front and slowly undo them.

Brooke shrugs the shirt off, and now we're skin to skin, only her satin bra between us. Her breasts are as full and beautiful as I remember. I undo the hooks in back and catch the weight of one breast in my hand.

She lets her bra drop, kissing me while I run my thumb over her skin.

I remember every inch of her, like the tiny mole

above her right nipple, and another on her shoulder. I kiss both. Brooke exhales as I lick them too.

"Are we really doing this?" she asks in a low voice.

"I think so." I kiss her lips then let her go. "Hang on a sec." I retrieve the bottle of port and glasses from the counter. "Don't want to waste it."

Brooke's grin makes me want to drop the wine and take her to the floor. I return the grin and follow her out of the living room through the hall to her bedroom. Watching her bare back and shapely ass under her shorts is a fine thing.

Her bedroom is a mess, the blankets on her bed rumpled, clothes on the floor. She must have taken every shirt and pair of shorts she owns and tossed them against the wall.

She shakes out the blankets, smoothing them, and sits on the bed. I take a moment to admire my lovely Brooke, who's leaning on one hand, before I plop down beside her. I pour the port, thumping the bottle to the nightstand.

"To us," I say, and we click glasses again. A much better toast than the one we'd started with. I'm also happy we're drinking this port and not the pinot noir Simon gave me. I want this to be about Brooke and me, no one else.

"I thought you were hungry." Brooke slants me a sly glance. "At the house you said you were starving."

"I am. But for something different now." I sip the satisfying port.

Brooke's glance turns even more mischievous, and she upends her glass all over my chest.

The next thing I know, I'm on my back with her licking the port off me. I'm laughing and groaning, trying to hold her while she works.

She lifts her head, all smiles, her hair coming out of its tight braid and damp with wine. Then she dumps the port onto *her* chest, and spreads her arms.

I love my playful Brooke, always have. I had to teach her to play, but she was a good student.

Brooke squeals with laughter as I roll over her, my tongue getting busy. She's tugging at my shorts now, wanting them off.

I make her wait until I've licked every drop from her, then I back off the bed and drop my shorts. I go ahead and do my underwear and shoes to save time later.

Here I am. Naked and unashamed, with my cock straight out to proclaim what's on my mind.

Brooke reaches out and strokes me from tip to balls.

"Gah." I curl my hands. I want to savor this time with her, because I may never be near her again, not like this, naked and wanting.

But all I can picture is me swan diving onto the bed and making hard and fast love to her. Brooke will squirm and laugh, and I'll come in thirty seconds.

Speaking of that ... I turn and snatch up my shorts, digging through the pockets. There's my wallet and inside, a condom, brand new and ready to go. I hold it up in triumph.

Brooke cocks a brow. "Oh, great. Why are you so prepared? Did you plan this?"

My face heats. "How could I have planned this? No, this is Ben's fault. He barges into my office after he starts going out with Erin and tells me I have to always carry a condom in my wallet. It's a long story ..."

"Because you convinced *him* to carry one." Brooke shakes her head at my surprised expression. "I know. Abby told me. Erin told her."

I imagine the ladies whispering about us and laughing, and my self-consciousness rises. "No secrets in this family."

"Are you going to put it on, or stand there and hold it?"

Before I can answer, Brooke leans to me and licks where her fingertips have touched.

"Uh ..." My eyes close and I lose the thread of the conversation.

The condom leaves my fingers. I hear foil rip and then feel the wet material brush my cock. Brooke's skilled hands unroll it up my shaft, sheathing me.

"I guess that answers that," I say in a strangled voice.

"Austin." Brooke stands up. She slides off her sandals, then unbuttons her shorts and shimmies out of them as she steps to me.

I expect her to continue speaking, but once she says my name, she falls silent. Our laughter dies away, and I kiss her.

Before this, we'd been playing, seeing how far we'd

take things. Now she's warm in my arms. Brooke's eyes close as she kisses me, and I know I'm in the right place in the universe.

I gently guide her back to the bed, and we fall upon it.

Chapter Seven

Brooke

I'M BREATHLESS AND SCARED, but also happy. Austin's mouth is hot on mine, his hands finding my every curve.

He always brings out the recklessness in me. I'm collected and buttoned-up most of the time—have to be —but Austin tears that away. He makes me want to do things like lick his cock, help him put on a condom, and then welcome him into my bed.

He's over me now, his warm weight familiar. I've missed it. Austin braces himself on his fists and gazes down into my eyes. I slide my hand between us and guide his cock to me.

My head goes back as he slips inside. For a moment, we lie still, feeling, remembering. Something changes when you make love with a person, and it changes between us now. Whatever fragmented us is still out there, waiting, but at this moment the pieces of us coalesce, merging into what we once were.

Austin's face relaxes, passion erasing tautness. We're together as I've dreamed, as I've longed for. He glides a little further inside, loosening the last of my anger and restlessness.

Making up with Austin is always a hell of a ride.

Austin smiles down at me, something wicked lighting his eyes. Then he goes for it.

All the way out, all the way in. I catch the rhythm and rise to him, the two of us grappling, holding, making furious love.

I laugh for the joy of it. Austin's smile widens, his desire swelling my heart with excitement. We rock and ride, my legs lifting, my feet closing around his very fine ass.

The sky is dark outside my window, the long summer day over. Inside it's roasting, Austin and I searing the air. Our bodies are slick with sweat, hot where we join. He cups my breast, two fingers lifting my nipple. I hold him close, and he drives into me in desperation.

Dark waves of ecstasy sweep me up. I hear myself shouting—his name, plus I think I yell that I love him, but he's making so much noise, he doesn't hear.

I peak right before he does. I close my eyes, my body one tight point as a flood of euphoria threatens to drown me.

Austin shudders, his body suddenly cool with sweat, and he hoarsely whispers my name.

We're holding each other as though we need to become one, our incoherent cries growing fainter until we crash down together. The waves recede, leaving us breathless on the shore that is my lumpy bed.

Austin

I DON'T WANT THIS TO END. I LIE BESIDE BROOKE, catching my breath, running a hand through my drenched hair. She snuggles in beside me. No shoving me out of her bed, no remorse, no anger.

Brooke has never used lovemaking to manipulate or win an argument. Sex for her is about the sex, about loving and enjoying. She leaves all our hang-ups and squabbles outside the bed and concentrates on love-making alone, squeezing as much pleasure out of it as she gives to me.

It's one of the reasons I fell in love with her.

I realize as I lie here that I'm in love with her still. And I don't want to let her go again.

Well, crappity crap.

Brooke strokes my chest with her skilled touch. "Still hungry?"

"Yeah, but feasting on you has helped."

"We could go somewhere." She scrunches her face

comically. "Not back to my parents' house. They'll all know what we sneaked away to do."

"To work things out?" I suggest.

"To have sex." Brooke laughs softly and lays her head on my shoulder. "That's what we mostly do."

"Between arguments, you mean."

"No." More gentle caresses. "It was good, Austin. A large part of what we had was good. We just both have egos. And stubbornness."

I don't want to say anything that will have us off this bed and back in the living room yelling at each other. "That's true," I agree.

What I wish I could say was that we have to find a way to make our stubbornness work for us. As in, make sure neither of us wants to leave again.

I love you, Brooke Marsh. How do I tell you that?

"How about this?" Brooke rises on her elbow. "A truce tonight. We'll clean up, go for some dinner. See what happens."

My heart beats faster in hope. "Okay," I say, as though it doesn't matter.

She kisses me. I touch her cheek, our kiss warm with afterglow.

We pry ourselves from the bed and into the shower in her bathroom. That leads to more play, and we bring each other to life with our hands. Brooke has never been shy with me, at least not after the first time we truly let loose.

We finally finish when the hot water depletes, and we emerge, breathless and rubbery legged.

I dry her off, and Brooke does me, which threatens to derail us again. Finally we gather our clothes, straighten our hair, and head out.

I like her next to me in my small car, where I can reach out and touch her. She rests her fingers on my knee, and I cover her hand with mine.

So comfortable, as though we've never been apart. The barrier between us hovers beyond our afterglow, but for now, it stays distant.

We go to Mason's, a great burger place that's crowded tonight. We have to wait for a table, but it's fine sitting at the bar, sipping wine until they're ready for us. Mason's isn't fine dining, but everything they serve is good. Brooke and I soon face each other over a small table for two and enjoy the food.

"I'm famished." I start putting away my burger, and Brooke doesn't exactly take dainty bites. "I'm not used to this."

"Sex?" Brooke leans closer to whisper. "Or great food?"

"S-e-x." I spell it out, as though no one will understand but us. "It's been a while."

Brooke drags a roasted potato through the juice on her plate. "How long?" She asks the question nonchalantly, but her eyes hold uneasiness.

"I can't say exactly." I set down my burger and lick my fingers. "You should know, though. You were there."

Her brows shoot upward. "What are you talking

about? You went out with other women after we split up."

"*Went out* with them." I wipe my fingers with my napkin. "Didn't go home with them."

Brooke stares at me, dumbfounded. "Are you telling me you've not slept with a woman in a year and change?"

"Yep. Couldn't conjure the interest. Dancing and joking around is one thing. Getting serious between the sheets, something else. What?" I continue as her mouth remains open. "You don't believe a guy can go a year or so without sex? We can. I'm not an animal. If I'm not into a woman, I'm not going to do it. Not fair to her or me. Besides, my heart wasn't in it. It was broken."

Brooke sits up. "Now you *are* shitting me."

"Don't you think that if I had slept with all kinds of women, I'd make sure you knew it? To show you I was over you?" I start to lift my burger but set it down again. "What about you? How many guys have you been with? Please don't tell me Simon is one of them."

"No." Her voice turns hard. "No one."

I lounge back in my chair. "Huh."

"*Huh*, what?"

"I guess you and me never really broke up. We didn't call each other for a year and a half, but neither of us started another relationship. We were in a holding pattern. Conclusion—we're still together."

"Wait, wait, wait. How do you figure that?"

"Think it through. We never officially called it quits. We just got mad and stormed away. I still have stuff at your house—unless you burned it. The stuff you left with me is carefully folded in a drawer. Though you probably don't want those clothes anymore. A couple years out of style."

Brooke eats another potato, chewing slowly. "I didn't burn anything."

"What's that?" I lean closer as though I hadn't heard her.

"I kept your stuff. It's in a box."

"Not as good as a drawer, but all right. Thank you. See? We've simply been taking a time out. We're still together."

I flash her my best grin as my heart thumps. This is too dangerous. She can throw the words back at me and tell me to get lost. She can always call her brother for a ride home.

"Let me think about this," she says.

"You do that. Except please don't take another year and a half."

"I'll think about that too."

"And don't break up with me right this minute, either. I'd lose my appetite, and my burger is too good for that."

To my relief, Brooke gives me one of her warmest smiles. "Truce, remember? For the rest of tonight, those topics are off limits. We'll enjoy our food and our wine."

"Maybe the rest of the port later?"

"Maybe."

We share another long look. Good thing the tables

are well spaced in this restaurant—this conversation is seriously personal.

After dinner, I drive her back home. I'm bracing myself to say good night and leave her, when Brooke says softly, "Come in. Let's have some more port."

Chapter Eight

Austin

THE NEXT MORNING I drive Brooke back to her parents' house, where she's left her car. She insists she can have Cedric bring it to her, but I want the opportunity to apologize to the family for vanishing from their dinner when they and Cedric had invited me.

The truce between Brooke and me lasted through the night of exuberant sex—I didn't have any more condoms, so there was no penetration, but we had a lot of fun anyway.

The truce continues through breakfast, which I make, because Brooke doesn't cook. The only reason she has eggs and bread is because Cedric occasionally drops off groceries for her.

"You don't have to drive me," she repeats even as we get into my car.

"I want to. I owe them an apology. I don't want to

be the jerk who has his way with their daughter then leaves everyone to eat my dust."

"They won't think that," she says with confidence.

I shrug. "I'll make it quick."

When we reach the house, Brooke resolutely walks inside with me instead of rushing to her car and high-tailing it out of there.

Viola turns from the coffee pot as soon as Brooke leads me into the kitchen. "Good morning, you two. Coffee, Austin?"

"Sure, thanks."

I accept the cup. Through the patio doors I see Brooke's father, Craig, enjoying coffee outside. Brooke glances around as though she wants to be anywhere but here, but she also takes a cup and sits down at the large breakfast bar, hand straying to the newspaper next to her.

"Sorry we ran out on you last night," I begin to Viola. My cheeks grow warm, and I cover my awkward-ness with a sip of coffee. "I'll make it up to you. Somehow."

Viola chuckles. "I heard the yelling in the dining room. Then I see you driving off together. I was hoping that would happen."

Brooke jerks her attention from the headlines. "*Mom.*"

"You two need to work things out." Viola stirs sugar into her coffee. "So, did you work it out?"

"Yes," I say at the same time Brooke says, "No."

Viola looks back and forth between us. "Seems like you need a little more time to decide."

Gladly. If that time involves Brooke's hands and mouth all over me, or us laughing hysterically while we play silly games like strip poker in her bed, so much the better.

Viola winks at me and drifts to the patio to join her husband. She sinks into the chair next to Craig, reaching over to take his hand. Craig absently grasps it, two people so much in love they automatically gravitate toward each other.

I take another sip and set down my cup. "Guess I should go."

Brooke swallows, but doesn't protest. "Thanks for making me breakfast."

"Anytime. You need decent nutrition."

She shrugs. "I usually go out. I get nutrition from a restaurant."

"Home cooked is better. My dad taught us how, so …"

"Tell your parents hi for me when you see them."

"Sure." I clear my throat. "I'll let you know my decision about the Ghibli."

Brooke returns her gaze to the newspaper. "No pressure. You either want it or you don't."

For some reason, her reasonable words irritate me. "Like I said, I'm not a zillionaire. If I can make it work, I will."

She sends me a small smile, but the tension between us has returned. "I look forward to it."

And, just like that, we're back to being frenemies. I take one more drink of coffee, which is good, and set the cup down.

"See you, Brooke."

"See you, Austin."

I give her a once-over, recalling how we'd finished off the unused can of whipped topping she'd found in the back of her refrigerator last night. Her hair looked good spiked with whipped cream.

Brooke says nothing, gives nothing away, and I turn and leave her.

Truce over.

———

Sunday means dinner at the McLaughlin family home. I had toyed with the idea of inviting Brooke today, but her cool good-bye made me change my mind.

I go home, shower, put on fresh clothes. I'm slow, my mind on everything else, my usual energy gone.

I couldn't leave well enough alone, could I? I had to take up the challenge Brooke leveled at me after Zach's rehearsal dinner to visit her dealership. I believed, in my arrogance, that she'd run straight back to me as soon as I gave her the chance.

She's showed me this will not be the case. Maybe we're too different, too stubborn—although in the matter of stubbornness and drive, we're a lot alike. Brooke works hard, is ambitious. And kick-ass. When she started as a salesgirl at the dealership, no one believed she knew anything about a combustion engine or how to calculate an interest rate, and now, she'll own the dealership.

I also work hard, but I'm content with what I have. I'm not eager to take over the business when Mom and Dad retire. I'll keep working there, and Ryan will be the big boss. Fine by me—he can deal with the problems. I'm good at schmoozing for effective advertising placement at the best price, and at keeping our suppliers and contractors happy. I'll keep on doing it, because I enjoy it.

I think Brooke overdoes her business life, and she believes I'm not enterprising enough. Maybe she's right.

I'll have to be very enterprising if I want to buy this car. I'm truly interested, not only because the Maserati is an amazing automobile, but it will remind me of Brooke. If I can't have her, I can at least have something to remind me of our great times together.

Most of the family is at the house today: Mom and Dad, Ryan and Calandra, Ben and Erin, Great Aunt Mary with her boyfriend, Andrew. Abby and Zach are on their honeymoon, and no one's heard from them except a quick "We're here in Santa Fe. We're fine" text.

I assume that with all the excitement of having Zach and Abby married off, Ben and Erin engaged, and Calandra and Ryan expecting, no one will talk much to me or about me.

I assume wrong.

"I heard you and Brooke were at Mason's last night," Ryan opens with as we gather around the dinner table. He knows everyone in town, and probably the manager of Mason's called him to relay the interesting news. "Is that anything?"

I'd told Brooke's mother yes, but now I say firmly, "No."

I'm not let off that easy—I have to tell them everything. So I launch into a truncated version of the story, starting with me test-driving the car, Cedric inviting me to dinner, Brooke and I arguing at said dinner, Brooke and I taking our fight away from her family's house so we won't disturb anyone. I gloss over the part about having sex with her, and say we'd ended up at Mason's. It had been good to talk without all the yelling.

Not one person at that table believes I haven't had sex with Brooke, but at least they keep quiet. For now, anyway. I know I'll catch it at the office tomorrow, where Mom can't be everywhere, glowering my brothers to silence.

After supper, I corner Ryan. It's hot though it's about nine in the evening, and we stroll near the pool. I can always strip off my shoes and step down into the water if I get too warm.

"I need some advice, big brother," I say.

"About Brooke?" Ryan glances across the yard and through the lighted windows at his wife, who is laughing at something Great Aunt Mary has said. His eyes shine with the love in his heart. "My advice is to let her do whatever she wants with you. Worth it. Trust me."

Sure, like Ryan and Calandra never had problems at all. The two of them had sometimes been as volatile as Brooke and me, though not quite in the same way. Ryan and Calandra had been together since childhood, and had a bond no one could break. They'd had to work through some shit before they found a common happiness, but they'd started from a solid place. What solidity did Brooke and I have?

"Not about Brooke," I say quickly.

Ryan raises his brows in perplexity. "What then?"

"This effing car." I let my shoulders slump. "I can't bring myself to tell Brooke I can't buy it—and I do want to buy it. But I can't make it work unless I put down a boatload of money. I have *some* funds tucked away, but not a boatload. Even if I sell my car or they'll take it in trade, it won't be enough. Unless Mom and Dad suddenly give me a ginormous raise." I send him a feigned hopeful look. Ryan is technically my manager, and he can run interference with our parents.

Ryan laughs. "Yeah, that's not going to happen. I'd help you out, bro, but all my finances are going to the kid." His smile spreads, his pride almost comical. It's also touching.

"I'm not asking you for money. I'm asking if you have any ideas on how I can get some."

"Loan shark? No, I'm kidding." Ryan lifts his hands as though he fears I'll run off searching for one on the spot. "Sell your body? Kidding again."

"Thanks a lot."

Ryan grows serious. "I don't understand why you're hung up on this car. If you can't afford it, buy something else. Or nothing. What you drive is plenty good."

"I know. It's ... I don't know ... symbolic."

"As in, if you can figure out how to buy the car, you can figure out how to win back Brooke?"

"Could be." I'm growing morose. "Or I could man up and tell her I'm dreaming. I'll back off, save my money, and try again later."

Ryan studies me. "I see—the responsible tactic. Show her you can be reasonable and realistic."

"Yeah, 'cause that always excites a woman."

"It does, in fact." Ryan again glances at Calandra, who is animated and smiling. "Women might drool over daring and dramatic guys, but when real life hits, they prefer someone who's solid as a rock, who will hold them up when they fall and keep the bad people away."

"A protector, you mean."

"Sure, you can put it that way."

"Huh. I tried to protect Brooke, and she shoved me away so fast I fell on my ass. Metaphorically."

Ryan's expression turns reflective. "There's a difference between protecting and smothering. A fine line. I had to learn it."

I let out a breath. "I know. I do too. I probably weigh her down like a wool blanket in August."

"What you do is show her you're choosing the sensible path. That you aren't looking at the Maserati because you thought buying it would help her out, and you've decided not to flash around money you don't have."

"Wait a minute." I pat my pockets as though searching for pen and paper. "I need to write all this down."

Ryan grins. "Don't bullshit me. Or her. Let things take their course with Brooke. She's not a woman who wants guys to impress her. She wants them to be themselves."

He had Brooke's character right, I had to admit. Brooke wasn't bowled over by Simon Lethbridge and his casual wealth, his car collection, his wine. She'd seemed bored by him and instead went to a burger joint with me. That's a point in my favor.

"Don't try to impress her," I repeat. "I think you have something there. Though I'm calling you on *Let things take their course*. I remember what you went through to finally win Calandra."

Ryan shrugs. "I did let things take their course—but I'm also king of the grand gesture. Remember how Ben proposed to Erin? That was me."

"You told him to do that?" I recall how Ben, my introverted older brother, bared his soul in front of an entire theater crowd.

"Ben worked out the details. I told him to tailor the gesture to Erin, what she loved, what she needed." Ryan's smile broadens. "What she couldn't resist."

I see Erin through the windows, standing very close

to Ben. As we watch, he cradles her against him, and she rests her head on his shoulder.

"What Brooke needs," I repeat softly. "What she can't resist."

"Yep."

I throw one arm around Ryan's shoulders and squeeze, feeling better than I have in a long while. "Thanks, big brother. You're the best."

I turn away and make for the back gate and my car. "Aw," Ryan's voice floats after me. "You're just saying that. 'Cause it's true."

———

"Hey," I say to Brooke. It's later, and I'm at home, lying on my bed, my feet propped on the footboard. I call her, and lo and behold, she answers.

"Hey." Her voice is soft, focused on mine. She's not distracted by work, the TV, other guys ... At least, I hope not other guys.

"I might come and see you tomorrow," I say. "At lunch, of course. Mom would not be happy if I ditched during work hours."

"I'll be working too."

"I know." I sound amazed. "It's like I read your mind."

Brooke laughs, and I wish I was next to her to catch her laughter with my lips. "I'm not always in the showroom on my lunch hour," she says. "I sometimes meet with clients."

"Or drive cars to them. I know." I rub my eyes and try not to picture her on her bed, wearing nothing but her silken bra and panties. Or maybe a sexy teddy. No, I *won't* think of that, because I'll never sleep. Or walk. Or think. "I'll show up on the off chance."

"Okay. If I'm not there, you can always talk to Mike."

"Mmm, not really what I had in mind."

"I meant if you have questions about the car."

I've already made my decision regarding the Ghibli, but I prefer to face her in person. "Mike and I can shoot the breeze about cars, but I'll be thinking of you."

She laughs again, and now I envision her in nothing but the panties. Or maybe those vanish too. Crap, I'll never sleep now.

"You are such a shit," she says.

"That's me."

"Good night, Austin."

"Good night, Brooke."

She hangs up the phone and I click mine off. "I love you," I whisper.

BROOKE ISN'T THERE WHEN I ARRIVE AT THE showroom at half past twelve. I hadn't really expected her to be. My job doesn't have super-regular hours either—I never know when I'll have to take someone out to a meal or for drinks, or drive them to the airport

—anything to thank people whose business we truly appreciate.

Mike greets me. "Austin. Good to see you."

"And you. Brooke is out." A statement, not a question.

"Yep. She and Raymond went to lunch with a guy who's buying a custom-built Alpha Romeo. But she left everything with me."

"Yeah?" I'm not sure what "everything" he's talking about.

"Here you go." Mike fishes in his desk, emerging with a folder and a key fob. "Sign the last paper and that sweet Maserati is all yours." He holds up the key fob and drops it into my hand when I thrust it out in confusion. "Congratulations."

Chapter Nine

Austin

"I DON'T UNDERSTAND." I stare at the fob in my hand, feeling its weight. The trident symbol of Maserati grins up at me.

"What's to understand?" Mike asks. "She's all yours. Well, after you sign this last sheet to accept the loan and make sure your insurance covers the Ghibli as soon as it's off the lot."

Mike pops open the folder, moving his tie out of its way, and hands me a pen. He's smiling like a proud father, a bit like Ryan, in fact.

"I came in here to tell Brooke I wouldn't be taking the car." My words are wooden, my fingers stiff.

Mike's brow furrows. "Not taking it? But your down payment already cleared."

"Down payment?"

Mike flips sheets in the folder. His expression has

changed to one of pity, as though I've entirely lost my mind and he has to be kind to me.

"There." Mike points. "One down payment."

I gaze blankly at the form that shows a hefty dollar amount and then the remaining price of the car plus the name of the bank that's floating the loan. It's my bank but I don't remember asking them to start anything. Or writing a check for that much money.

"This is weird." I stare at the page as though the ink will evaporate if I gaze at it long enough, then lift my head. "I'm going to be honest with you. I didn't make this payment."

Mike peers at me in concern. "Well, someone did. One of your family, maybe? To surprise you?"

I might have thought so, but not after my talk last night with Ryan. He isn't about to part with a dime now that he has a wife and child on the way, and I wouldn't let him even if he wanted to. My brothers are in similar situations.

Or maybe ... My brothers collectively come through sometimes. On the other hand, they can't keep a secret worth shit. Not one of them looked guilty or excited at the office this morning, so I doubt they called Brooke and rushed her money for baby brother's car.

"Probably not," I say. I have another idea. I'm not certain why this person would help me out, but he might have an ulterior motive. A motive called Brooke.

"Let me sign," I say. If this benefactor wants to part with his money, fine by me.

I scribble my name on the relevant paper and then

call my insurance company to make certain all is squared away on their end. Because I'm responsible that way. Mike can tell Brooke how steady and dependable I am when she returns.

"Again, congratulations." Mike shakes my hand. "She's a beauty. Take good care of her, all right?"

"It'll end up in your shop if I don't." I cross my fingers when I say it. The car is amazing and I don't want a scratch on it.

Mike walks me out. The Ghibli has been washed and shined, the inside thoroughly cleaned. The mechanics come out to watch me get in and start it up. They love these cars too.

I want to shout my joy as I drive away, but I contain myself. This car is awesome, and if someone wants to score points with Brooke by making the down payment for me, I'll let him. And find a way to pay him back.

I drive south to the Encanto area and find Simon's house. He's home, in the garage, revving the Lamborghini.

"Austin," Simon sings out when he sees me. He unfolds from the car. "Listen to that. Isn't she beautiful? Ah, I see you have the Maserati. Brooke talked you into it."

"She did." I take in his roomy garage and the spy cameras and keypads. Simon might not have spent much on his small house, but his garage is like Fort Knox. "I have a favor to ask. I need to pump up security on my own garage. It's not bad, but this is a high-dollar car, and the number one crime in Phoenix is car theft."

"And you want some recommendations? I have great security guys. They know their stuff."

"I was thinking more ... Could you keep the car here overnight, or until I can increase my security? I'll pay rent if you want."

"Oh, that's a fine idea. No one will bother it here, and she'll be in good company." Simon looks over his small fleet with a gleam of satisfaction. This is one happy man.

"One question." I step into the shade of the garage and face him. Simon is about my height, and I can look him straight in the eye. "Did you give me a donation?"

His brows go up, and wariness enters his stance. "Pardon?"

"When I went to Brooke's showroom today, someone had paid the down payment on this car for me. Anonymously. I don't know many people with that kind of money to throw around, except you. And you seem generous."

Simon laughs. "Not *that* generous, mate. Someone really paid it for you? Your fairy godmother, perhaps?"

I stop, my thoughts rearranging themselves. I'd fixed on Simon because I remembered how he watched Brooke when she was here. He'd tried to impress her with his generosity by giving her the wine, which I knew was a highly expensive bottle. By making the down payment for the Ghibli, he'd help Brooke make a sale, plus enable her friend—me—to have a great car, earning her praise and making me pathetically grateful to Simon.

Another laugh, and then Simon grows thoughtful. "Wait, I know who did this."

I'm starting to figure it out, but I motion for him to continue.

"Brooke herself." Simon grins at me. "It's exactly the sort of thing she'd do."

The idea has been dawning on me once I realize how hilarious Simon finds the thought of *him* being my benefactor. Brooke has done this. Why?

To be a good friend? Or to show me she can? Was this a *No hard feelings* gesture or a *See how far I've come on my own?* statement?

"The dear girl." Simon shakes his head. "She'll do anything for a sale."

I snap my attention back to him, annoyed. "What does that mean?"

Simon's brows rise. "What it sounds like. Brooke isn't one to lose. She badgered me for months to buy this." He pats the top of the Lamborghini. "Well, I shouldn't say *badger*. Rather, she used gentle persuasion. But she never let up. And look, it's in my garage now, my name on the deed."

I don't like the way Simon smirks when he talks about Brooke. I might be reading him wrong, but the innuendo in his tone when he speaks of gentle persuasion makes my blood boil.

"I hope you're not disparaging the woman I intend to marry," I say stiffly.

Simon's smile vanishes, and he gapes at me.

I gape at myself. Where the hell did that come from?

Maybe it came from me finally admitting I love her. Brooke has always been the one for me.

Simon shakes his head as though to clear it. "You want to marry Brooke?"

"Yep."

"Wow." Simon gives me a look of undisguised admiration. "You lucky sod."

"I haven't asked her yet." My anger abates, as it's obvious Simon isn't an indignant rival. "She probably won't say yes. I'm going to have to convince her."

"Worth it, I'd say. You have balls, mate. I admit, I've wanted to ask her out, or to maybe have a fling, because ... well, she's beautiful. And has a personality. But marriage. That's a deep choice."

"Or a stupid one." I grin.

"No, I can see it. I did when you were both here, but I didn't want to admit it to myself. You two are good together. But that's me, an incurable romantic. Have to be, to love these cars, am I right? If there's anything I can do to help, just give me the word."

"I will." I drag in a breath, the dry heat of an Arizona June filling my lungs.

A grand gesture, Ryan said. One that is about Brooke, and about me. Something she needs, and something I can give her.

"Actually, there is one thing ..." I explain to Simon, and his face lights up. He grants my request and I leave him.

As I say goodbye to Simon and the Ghibli and wait for my cab to take me back to the showroom, I know what I'll do for Brooke. I'll need my brothers to help me, but this is something they'll get behind.

I'll do it whether it makes her accept me or not, because she does need it.

What the hell? I'll take my shot. When it involves Brooke and me, I never say never.

———

Brooke

BECAUSE I'M RUNNING ALL OVER THE VALLEY keeping customers happy, I miss Austin both times he's at the showroom. I know it's twice, because Mike tells me.

"He seems happy with the car," Mike says when I return, breathless and exhausted from my second errand. "But confused. Wondering who made the payment for him. You handled that paperwork." He leaves the statement open, wanting me to fulfill his curiosity.

"Confidential," I say. Mike is crestfallen but takes it in stride.

"Sure thing, boss."

I return home by seven, change into sloppy shorts, T-shirt, and flip flops, put my feet up, and enjoy a glass of cold water.

I don't hurry when someone knocks on the door.

Could be the neighbor kids selling everything under the sun for their band or sports group or chess club. I can always be counted on to buy something.

I open the door, putting on my best nice-neighbor face. That façade cracks as soon as I see Austin on the doorstep, silhouetted against the red and gold sky.

"Hello," I say neutrally.

He simply looks at me.

I can get lost in Austin's eyes, but this evening I can't read what's in them. I know he knows what I did, but I can't tell how he feels about it.

I furnished the down payment because I'd seen Austin's longing for the Ghibli, his resignation and wistfulness when he'd concluded he couldn't afford it. He never directly stated to me that he couldn't, but his expression said it all. I wanted to give the car to him to bring back his sparkle. Austin wholeheartedly enjoys things, and I want to see that again.

I open the door wider. "Want to come in?"

Austin steps inside, but instead of heading for the living room, he halts against me. Again, he says nothing, only studies me in silence.

"Wine?" I ask nervously.

Austin lifts his hand from behind his back, showing me a paper wine bag with a bottle inside. "Brought my own."

"Great." My mouth is dry in spite of all the ice water I've just drunk. "Glasses are in the kitchen."

"They can wait."

Austin remains unmoving, his warmth welcome

even in the summer heat. He doesn't kiss me or touch me, only locks my gaze with his.

"Nice to see you," I say softly. I'm not lying—my body is burning with his nearness. I haven't seen him since yesterday, and I miss him.

"Why?" he asks.

I understand what he's talking about. "Because you really like the car."

Austin's eyes close briefly then open again. "Doesn't mean I expected you to buy it for me."

"I didn't buy it. I only helped. As a friend."

Austin finally shuts the door behind him, closing out the heat of the night.

"I have some very good friends, including my brothers," he says. "And they wouldn't have done that for me."

I pry the wine from his grasp and head nervously to the kitchen. "I wanted to."

Austin follows me, leaning on the breakfast bar while I locate glasses, just as he had Saturday night. "And I asked why. It ate up any commission you might have earned from the sale."

"I don't care about the commission. I didn't sell the car to you for that." The wine is another very good pinot noir, a *grand cru* from the Côte de Nuits region of Burgundy, and I have the feeling I know where he obtained it.

"To mark it off your balance sheet?"

"Austin." I thump the bottle to the counter and regard him impatiently. "You love that car—it was *made* for you—and I wanted you to have it. I have a nice chunk of savings, and if I decide to use it to help a friend buy a Maserati, that's my business."

The corners of Austin's mouth twitch, but I can't tell whether he's angry or not. "You do this for all your friends?"

"No. The special ones only."

"Ah, so I'm special to you?"

I reach for the corkscrew but set it on the counter. "You always have been." I look straight at him. "Always will be."

Austin stills, his lips parted, as though he'd been about to throw me a snappy comeback.

When he says nothing, I peel the seal from the top of the bottle and insert the corkscrew. My corkscrew's not a fancy device—it opens the bottle, and that's all I need. The wine flows into the glasses, a translucent dark red.

"Did you come here to yell at me about the car?" I set a glass in front of him. "I guess red goes with that."

"No." Austin ignores the glass. "To thank you."

"Oh."

I don't know how else to respond. I'd wondered how he'd react to my spontaneous gift—I pictured everything from elation to fury and refusal to accept it.

I wasn't expecting him to gaze at me, his face impassive, while he quietly expressed his gratitude.

I lift my full glass. "You're welcome." I sip, savor. "You got this from Simon."

"Yes. He thought I should celebrate owning a new car."

"You spoke to him?" Of course he had—how else would he have picked up the wine? My brain and my mouth aren't working together.

"He's babysitting the Ghibli in his high-tech lockup."

"Oh." My responses are brilliant. "That was smart."

"Nice of him," Austin says.

"Yeah, Simon's a nice guy."

"I don't really want to talk about Simon."

I take another sip of wine. "Me either."

Austin reaches over the counter, takes my glass from me, and sets it down. He comes to me, and as he had at the front door, steps close and studies me.

"What?" I whisper.

"Tell me one more time why you made sure I could buy the car."

It's easy. I don't have to think about it or pretend I have a complicated motive.

"Because I saw how happy it made you, and I want you to be happy." *Because I love you. I've never stopped.*

"It's not the car that makes me happy." Austin cups my face. "It's you."

I part my lips to say, *Oh*, again. Austin tilts my head up and leans to take my mouth in a slow, thorough kiss.

Chapter Ten

Brooke

UNLIKE SATURDAY, when we ripped each other's clothes off, Austin and I undress each other leisurely.

We're in my bedroom—which I straightened on the off chance we'd end up here again one day—he sliding my T-shirt off.

He's still in office clothes, a button-down shirt and tie. I work my fingers under the tie's knot and loosen it, then pull apart the silken ends until it's slithering from him. I unfasten his shirt, one button at a time, while he carefully unhooks my bra.

Even when we're standing against each other, skin touching, Austin kisses me unhurriedly, savoring me like I'd savored the pinot.

I rest my hands on his back, enjoying the play of muscles there. Austin has always been so strong. He dances, he jogs, he works out, keeping himself honed.

It's a pleasure to touch his smooth skin and steely body.

He touches me as well, hands gliding down my spine to my hips and waist. He cups my breasts, thumbs teasing me to life, sending fire through my blood.

"There is nothing in the world more beautiful than you," he murmurs. Austin kisses the shell of my ear, his breath hot.

He's busy undoing the drawstring of my running shorts. I wrestle a little with his belt and then unfasten his pants.

Austin takes a step back to rid himself of shoes, the pants, and his underwear, coming back to me in nothing but his socks.

He pushes my shorts and underwear away, and now we're naked together, our mouths meeting as leisure gives way to fever. Our kisses heat up as we touch, stroke, relearn each other.

Austin trails kisses down my neck and to my breasts. He eases his rush as he suckles me, making me groan. I arch to him, my fingers in his hair as he feasts on me.

His hand slides between my legs. His palm is hot, and I rub myself on him, unable to stop. Austin smiles as he kisses me again, knowing he's driving me crazy.

I close my fingers around his cock, liking it when he gasps. "Damn, woman."

"Hey, I can make you happy too."

"I'd say you can." Austin straightens up,

unashamedly enjoying what I'm doing. I stroke and squeeze, while Austin sucks in a shuddering breath.

His hands land on my shoulders, though he gentles his grip for me. He steers me to the bed, and soon we're on it, kissing, licking, nipping, working each other up until we're wild with longing. He breaks from me only to dive for his pants, returning with a condom.

"I came packing," he says breathlessly. "Decided to never leave home without one."

"Good thinking."

I help him put on the condom, then we spend a moment studying each other before he rolls me down into the blankets, and slides inside me.

I love Austin. I know it with all my heart as I look into his beautiful eyes. He's funny and fun, one of the few people who can make me laugh. I'm intense, but he eases me down, teaching me how to relax and imbibe the pleasures of life. He points out my arrogance yet makes me believe I can do anything I wish.

Austin makes a soft sound, and his thrusts speed up. The sensation shatters my thoughts. I wrap myself around him and hang on.

"Brooke." His voice is breathless. "Damn, you make me insane."

I try to answer, but I can only cry wordlessly as Austin takes me over the top.

His shouts meld with mine. We slam together, gripping each other, kissing, crying out. He pounds the bed with a fist, and I press my fingers to his tight body.

We come together, and ride our passion until the

end, when we land breathlessly in a pile of limbs and laughter.

————

Austin and I share the bottle of wine in bed. We toast Simon, who has provided us another fine wine to drink together.

This time, I don't pour the wine on myself and Austin so we can lick each other clean. It's tempting —Austin tasted great flavored with port—but I decide to be dignified ... as dignified as I can be sitting naked in bed drinking from a wide-bowled wineglass.

"What do we do now?" I ask softly as we rest side by side, imbibing the last of the wine.

"Hmm, let me think." Austin pretends to ponder. "Have more sex?"

I laugh. We've done it three times by now. When Austin claimed to be packing condoms, he wasn't kidding. He'd brought a box.

"I mean after that."

"Um—"

I touch my fingers to his lips before he can say *Have more sex* again.

"Are we back together?" I ask.

Austin lifts my hand away. "No."

My heart sinks, sadness pulling at me. I must look dejected, but I can't disguise it.

Austin touches the corner of my mouth. "We never

broke up, remember? So we're not *back* together. We're *still* together."

My dejectedness evaporates. "You have everything figured out, don't you?"

"Yep." Austin caresses my cheek. "I do understand now why you didn't want me interfering with your life. It took me a while to figure it out, but I have—believe it or not. You needed to achieve things no one handed to you, and I was hindering you as much as those trying to block you. I thought I was helping, and it made me furious that you didn't realize that. And I didn't make things easy for you bursting in like a grizzly defending his mate. I understand why you were mortified, but I thought I was doing the right thing."

"I know you did." I get that now. "But I was scared and angry, and tired of people treating me like a simple-minded little girl who couldn't do anything on her own. Plus you did nearly get me fired."

"I regret that—trust me. I came off as being a macho jerk, right? Will it help if I told you I apologized to those guys?"

I blink in surprise. "You did? When was this?"

"About a week after. Raymond told me where they hung out, and I met with them. They were total assholes and totally in the wrong, but I didn't want anything I did to blow back on you. I got them to be calm and get over it. A few beers didn't hurt. They admitted you were good at your job and knew you'd kick their butts in sales. Ryan—who knows everyone— said a friend of his was hiring at another dealership and

I sent them there. I apologized to Raymond too, by the way."

I listen with my mouth open, but the deed sounds just like Austin. He's forever keeping the peace, charming everyone, even total assholes. He'd made the apology for my sake, I understand, not worrying about what those guys thought of *him*.

"Thank you." I twine my hand through his. "That was good of you. If I'd known that I might have climbed down from my high horse long ago. Maybe." I could be a stubborn idiot.

Austin shrugs. "I didn't want you to think I was still interfering, so I asked Raymond not to say anything." He lets out a breath. "I admit I did worry that you couldn't make it on your own. A stupid thing happens to guys when they're enchanted by a beautiful woman. They start to forget she's a person underneath, can't quite believe she can think for herself. We become knights-errant who want to save the damsel. Never mind she doesn't care about being saved."

I ponder that. "I don't know if it's the wine or that I'm very happy being with you, but I'm taking it as a compliment you think I'm so beautiful it erases my brains."

"Of course." Austin wraps a wisp of my hair around his forefinger. "What being away from you made me realize is that you are the whole package. A smart, capable woman who doesn't need me. It scared me that you didn't need me. That meant I could lose you anytime. Easily."

"I *do* need you." I snuggle closer to him. "I need the Austin who makes me laugh and lets me unleash my wild side. You show me how to enjoy things like fine wine and the joy of riding in a well-made car. I live in a crappy house and focus on my work, while your house is tailored to you—made to hold the things you love."

"Yeah, it's not bad." Austin dismisses my assessment, but I know I'm right. He glances around my room. "I was going to be nice and say this place has potential if we try, but I think it should be torn down and the parts given away to our charity—if any are salvageable. Most will have to be a landfill donation."

"Thanks a lot." I huff, but secretly agree.

Austin had once told me I'd taken this house so I could avoid living. I'd been annoyed, but now I believe he's hit upon a truth. It's easy to stay at work and concentrate on it if home is uncomfortable and lonely.

"Okay," I say. "We've decided I don't know shit about how to pick out a house, and you don't know how to handle a successful businesswoman. Where does that leave us?"

"At the moment?" Austin takes in the mostly empty bottle and the dark window over my bed. It's nearing midnight. "That leaves us with a great wine and spectacular sex. And celebrating the fact that we never broke up. I think that's pretty good for one night."

I could argue, say we need to work through a lot more before we're a couple again.

But I don't care. I've missed the hell out of Austin, and I do need him in my life. Not in a clingy way, but to bring out the best in myself. He needs me too—I hope—to share his triumphs and his sorrows.

Austin *is* like me in that he wants to prove himself. He's the youngest McLaughlin and considered the screwup, but the fact that McLaughlin Renovations is known throughout the Valley shows he's not. Their name is in every local magazine I open, at every home show, and on bus stops and billboards throughout town, plus signs in front of plenty of houses where they've been hired. Austin knows what the hell he's doing. And like I said, he knows how to keep the peace.

Tonight this is about Austin and me. Not success or failure, or cars, or wine, or living the good life, or just getting through a day.

It's about us, and love, friendship, and new understanding. I reach for him and pull him down to me, showing him how happy I am that he walked back into my life.

Austin

IN THE MORNING—AFTER A LITTLE MORE SEX, OF course—I leave Brooke's house.

For the next couple of weeks, I make myself stay away from her.

I don't want to, but my grand gesture won't work unless I absent myself for a while. I want her to be truly surprised.

I call her, and she calls me, but I'm evasive about when I want to get together again. She's puzzled and not happy—though she says nothing—but I'll make it up to her.

I'm a little worried that me vanishing might make Simon think he can leap in and steal her, but whenever I mention him to Brooke, I can tell she doesn't give a rat's ass about Simon or his money. He's a client, a nice guy, and a sort of friend. That's it.

I have to recruit my brothers, of course, for my grand gesture. They're all for it. Though I've had the seeds of this project in place for a long time, I need the family to help me pull it together quickly.

During the chaos, Zach and Abby return from their honeymoon.

"So you and Brooke hooked up?" Zach asks me in the lunchroom on his first day back. He's tanned and relaxed, like he's figured out his place in life. The way he and Abby kissed before heading into their respective offices tells me why.

Zach's teasing me, because when he and Abby first got together, I said almost the exact same thing to him.

"Yep." No hiding it. I pour another cup of coffee. I've drunk a lot of it trying to keep myself from Brooke. Wine makes me think of her, so I haven't touched a drop since the bottle we shared in her bed. "Hooked up several times. She bought me a car, and we decided we like each other again. That's about it."

Zach sends me a stern look. "You are leaving out a

hell of a lot, but I'm letting it go. Ryan will fill in the gaps—Calandra tells him everything Brooke tells her."

"Seriously, there is no privacy in this family." I strive to be disapproving but can't quite manage it.

"At least I won't be in your face asking you questions. *If* you give me a ride in that Maserati."

"Absolutely. We'll go all out and see what she can do."

"That's what I want to hear." Mom walks in on the last of our discussion. "My sons talking about recklessly driving a race car."

"I mean on a track, with lots of safety in place," I add quickly.

"Sure." Mom heads for the coffee machine, pausing to kiss Zach's cheek. "Welcome home, sweetie. I won't lecture you about the car, Austin, if you let *me* drive it."

I'm not surprised. Mom is not a timid person. "Whenever you want," I say. "Just give me the word."

"After you and Brooke are good," she says, and breezes out.

"I guess you'd better settle things," Zach says to me. "Congratulations."

"Don't congratulate me yet." I cradle my cup, my self-assurance sinking by the minute. "She might refuse everything and freeze me out. Or say thank you but go away."

Zach, basking in the glow from his honeymoon, claps me on the shoulder. "She'll accept. You two are great together."

"So says the man stupidly in love. Not everyone gets a happily ever after, you know."

"Yes they do," says stubborn Zach. "It's not exactly the same for everyone, and not everyone recognizes their happy ending when they have it. But it's there, even if it takes a while."

"Optimistic and romantic." I shake my head. "What happened to my cynical brother?"

"Abby found him." Zach's gaze goes to the show-room outside the open door, where Abby walks purposefully from her office to our mom's.

Abby pauses at Erin's desk to speak to her, and the two ladies share a laugh. Both are vibrant, attractive women. No wonder my brothers have turned into bright-eyed numbskulls.

I probably look just like them.

I make it through the rest of that week, catching Abby and Zach kissing in the break room only once, which has to be a record. I catch Erin and Ben too. It's a love nest in here.

At the end of the day on Friday, I drive home and fetch the Ghibli. Simon sent guys to my house to reinforce my garage and install a security system. Simon is quickly becoming a friend, now that he's stopped trying to land Brooke, though I'll keep my eye on him.

I drive to Brooke's dealership as she's leaving through the back door. The guys have let me in through the gate—they're becoming friends too.

Brooke pauses when she sees me. We haven't met

face to face for nearly two weeks, and I can tell she's not happy about that.

"Hey there." I step out of the car but keep it running. "Drive you home?"

"My car's here." Brooke gestures to one of the garages.

"It'll be safe until morning." Probably safer than at her own house. "Or I can bring you back for it later."

"Are you saying we need to talk?" Brooke's expression is wary. She looks hot today in a sunshine-yellow dress with red high-heeled sandals and red earrings.

"Nope. Driving you home, that's all. You can talk about whatever you want."

Brooke hesitates. She wants to turn me down, show me she's not bothered by the fact she hasn't seen me in person for two weeks.

But she's curious, I can tell, about what I've been up to. Plus she has more guts than any person I've ever known.

"All right." She saunters to the Ghibli as I race to open the door for her. "Drive me home. I can have Mike drop off my car later."

"Okay by me." I usher her in, Brooke as graceful as ever as she slides into the car.

I'm around to the driver's seat in no time flat. I wave at the guys who open the gate for me, and pull out, the engine purring.

Brooke examines the car as we go, Phoenix traffic slowing us to a crawl. She pushes buttons, adjusts her seat, and plays with all the controls she can reach.

"I don't always get the chance to check these out," she explains as I cock an eyebrow at her. "It's a great model. You look good in it."

"You've already sold me the car," I remind her. "Relax. Enjoy the ride."

"I am enjoying it." Brooke tunes my sound system, finding a station that plays music we both like.

We start singing along, matching harmonies. I'll take her to a club in this car—I picture the line of people watching in blatant envy as I pull up in my sexy ride with the most beautiful woman on earth on my arm.

Brooke is so interested in playing with the gadgets that she doesn't pay much attention to my route. I snake down Bethany Home and pull into an older neighborhood, halting before a brick bungalow with a wide yard and tall trees. The trees shade the house from the westering sun, sending coolness over us as I roll into the driveway.

Brooke looks around in surprise, but not alarm. She probably assumes I'm running an errand for McLaughlin Renovations. "Oh, cute house. Who lives here?"

I fish a key out of my pocket and hold it out to her. "You do."

____

Chapter Eleven

Brooke

I STARE at the keys in Austin's hand. He doesn't move, his face expressionless.

I'm not sure I heard him right. I dart a glance at the house. It's small and brick and old—that's all I know about historic houses. But it's adorable. The small porch has a roof that curves in a J-shape from gable to eave. The green front door is arched, and the brick walkway is lined with purple, pink, and scarlet vincas for summer.

I clear my throat, which is dry and parched. "What do you mean, it's mine?"

"Your name is on the deed. You'll need to sign some papers, but I thought you might want to look it over first."

"Look it over ..." I flick my gaze again at the house

and back to Austin. He's serious. "Why the hell are you giving me a *house?*"

"Because yours is crap," Austin says without blinking. "No offense."

I open and close my mouth a few times. "You can't buy me a house."

"You bought me a car."

"I didn't *buy* it for you, I—"

He stops my words with his fingers. "Will it make you feel better if I say I didn't *buy* this for you? We're always picking up properties no one wants. We got this at an auction when it was abandoned. I was already fixing it up for the hell of it, but I thought—who do I know who needs a house? Oh yeah. Brooke. At least I can offer it to her."

For some reason I need to keep arguing. "You can't. Your family will be out the money for the bid and the renovation—"

Again, Austin touches my lips. "I've already talked this over with them. Mom and Dad know you won't be thrilled taking a gift, so they said you can pay back the renovation cost with whatever you get from your house when you sell it. You know, if you decide to sell it and take this one."

Though Austin's voice is quiet, sincerity radiates from him.

Before our sort-of reconciliation, I'd have believed he was trying to one-up me for the down-payment I made for this car. Challenging me.

Today I'm reading that he genuinely wants me to

have this. That he's convinced his family the house will be perfect for me, to help me out.

I'm still uncertain, but I gently take the keys from his hand. "How about we go inside?"

Austin relaxes but only partly. He opens the detached garage's door with a remote and parks inside. He charges from the car and around to my door to escort me out, which makes me want to laugh.

He guides me to the house's front door, and I unlock it. Together we step inside.

I love the place immediately. The small entrance foyer has a stained glass door opening into the rest of the house. Beyond that a square hall leads to a living room, dining room, kitchen, and back porch, with a small staircase to a second floor. Soft white walls, cove molding, and wood accents greet me.

The kitchen is a single room, not a galley. The appliances are new, sparkling, and probably work far better than mine ever will. A large table sits in the middle like a kitchen island, with a couple of chairs pulled up to it.

I might decide to learn cooking if I can do it in this kitchen. Austin follows me in and starts talking up the appliances as though I know what any of his jargon means.

"You have a convection cooktop, with a warming burner in the back, and touch controls. French door refrigerator, and a farmhouse sink. And here ..." He opens a door about four inches thick and waves to a dark, deep cupboard. "Wine cellar. Or at least the closest thing to it. Plenty of slots for reds and a cooler to chill your whites."

Now *this*, I understand. I examine the cupboard and see several bottles of wine already in place.

"Don't tell me Simon gave you those." I touch a bottle of Côte de Rhone.

"Nope. These are from me."

Austin says it so quietly that I know he took time and trouble to pick out exactly what I'd like. For some reason, I tear up.

"What's upstairs?" I say brightly, shutting the door.

Austin leads me back to the hall. The other rooms are unfurnished, but I see possibilities. The living room has a fireplace, which will be cozy the few nights of the year it's cold enough to build one. The long porch in the back beckons, and I see chairs and a small yard with more cheerful flowers.

"Who put in the garden?" I ask.

"Mom thought it would be a good idea. Abby and Calandra picked out the flowers for you."

My heart warms even more. His whole family plus my best friends have been in on this.

Swallowing the lump in my throat, I ascend the staircase. At the top is a landing with a window looking out above the front door. Up here are two bedrooms, one with an attached bathroom, and a smaller bathroom off the landing. The largest bedroom has a view of the back garden, with a line of trees screening the house from the back-door neighbor.

There's a bed in this room, done up in white

comforters. The sun is setting, bathing everything in a golden glow.

"It's beautiful," I say softly.

"Glad you think so. Keep the keys. The house is yours."

I turn to him. Austin is silhouetted against the light from the window, his strength outlined.

"Why did you do this?" I ask. "The real answer."

"Because I thought you'd like it." Austin closes the distance between us, gazing down at me with his intense eyes. "You fit here."

"Like you fit with the car?"

"Exactly." Austin takes my hands and raises them to his lips. "I want you to have someplace to be happy."

I gape at him for a second, and then the tears well. "That's so wonderful. Why would you— After I— We—"

"Shh." Austin squeezes my hands. "This is a gift from one friend to another."

Now I'm bawling. I fling myself at him and hold him tight.

"*Oof.* Does this mean you want to stay?"

"Don't laugh." I pull away. "Stop being so wonderful, you... you... *shit.*" I snatch up a pillow from the bed and smack him with it. The pillow is so nice, that I hug it to myself.

Then he's hugging me, the pillow between us, as I kiss Austin. And kiss him.

When we finally draw apart, the pillow falls. Austin catches it and tosses it to the bed.

"Is there a reason the only piece of furniture in this house is a bed?" I ask, my whole body humming.

Austin shrugs. "You need a place to sleep. Plus, there's the kitchen table."

"A place to sleep and to eat. What more do I need?"

"My thoughts exactly."

I glance at the bed. "We should make sure it's comfortable."

"Guess we should."

Austin's grin melts everything cold left inside me. He's always been there for me, I realize, even if from afar. We never said good-bye when we'd broken up, maybe because we both knew in our hearts it wouldn't be forever. Somehow we'd gravitate to each other again, no matter how much we tried to stay away.

Austin understands what I need, and completes me in ways I never expected. I understand the parts of him he hides from everyone else—the compassionate, caring man he truly is.

For a moment, we regard each other, each with our own thoughts. Then I let out a growl and launch myself at him. Austin laughs and catches me in his arms.

Next, we're tearing each other's clothes off—literal tearing at some points—until we fall onto the welcoming bed. Austin remembered to bring condoms, of course. I've started carrying some too, just in case. We have fun getting him ready.

Now, Austin's on me, gazing down at me. I see the kindness in him, which he will forever deny, always pretending to be the goof. But he looks after everyone, even if they don't realize it.

"Austin," I whisper.

"Shh." He kisses me, probably thinking I want to argue more about the house.

"I need to tell you something."

"Later." Austin nibbles my neck, which is distracting, but I persist. If I don't say it, I'll regret it.

I touch his face, guiding him to look at me again. "I need to tell you now." I take a breath. "I love you."

Austin stills. Will he gape in horror and run away? Or laugh at me?

After a long, tense moment, Austin exhales and wipes his brow. "Whew! I'm glad you said that, because I was going to tell you I love *you*. I wasn't sure how you'd react."

"I wasn't sure how *you'd* react."

"Well, damn." He shakes his head. "We have *got* to stop being afraid to talk to each other."

I lace my arms around his neck. "Agreed."

"So." Austin gently kisses my lips. "How about I go next. I love you, Brooke."

"I love you, Austin." Now that I've said it, I like saying it. I look forward to saying it again.

"I'm going to tell you that every day," he says. "A couple of times, probably. Will that bother you?"

My heart is light, happy. "Not at all."

"Good. I'll probably yell it a few times in the next hour."

"Hour? Is that all?"

Austin growls, his eyes glinting. "Oh, you will pay for that, my love."

"Mmm. Sounds fun."

Austin clasps my wrists and kisses me, his weight sinking me into what is a very comfortable bed. He slides inside me and starts to love me, taking me rapidly into pure pleasure.

"I love you." Austin says it with low intensity. "Love you."

"I love *you*, Austin." I hold him, touch him, kiss him, and join with him until we're shouting the words at the tops of our voices.

We wind down, the house cradling us, and we whisper it as we drowse in our newfound understanding.

———

Austin

BROOKE IS BEAUTIFUL IN THE MORNING. I KNOW she won't believe me, so I say nothing, but I enjoy her mussed hair and sleepy face as she stumbles to the bathroom for a shower.

Abby, Erin, and Calandra, at my request, have stocked the bathroom with the right shampoo, conditioner, and other things Brooke uses. They had fun shopping for her.

"You thought of everything," Brooke's voice sings back to me.

"Me and my posse, yes."

Brooke pokes her head out the door. "Posse?"

I tuck my hands behind me and watch her. "Friends and family. People you know and love."

Her eyes fill. "Why is everyone being so nice to me?"

"I don't know. We love you?"

"Stop it." Brooke wipes her eyes. "I'm taking a shower now."

I see the invitation in her eyes, but if I join her, we'll be in there far too long, and she'll be embarrassed about what comes next. Last thing I want right now is Brooke embarrassed.

I wave her off, and once the door is closed, I dive out of bed.

I have a quick wash in the second bathroom, combing my hair and dressing with stuff from the overnight bag I'd stashed in the other bedroom. I have a change of clothes for Brooke too, courtesy of Calandra. I don't have time to shave, but I'll have to live with that.

I leave the bag in the master bedroom for Brooke and dash downstairs to fix coffee. The shelves in the kitchen are well stocked, and I start breakfast. I'll need to make a lot of food.

By the time the shower goes off upstairs, I'm up to my eyeballs in pancakes and bacon, toast and eggs. Brooke enters the kitchen not long later, dressed in shorts and a sleeveless top. She makes straight for the coffee I've brewed, and not until she's sipping does she realize how much I've cooked.

"I'm not *that* hungry," she says. "Though maybe you are."

She saunters over and laces one arm around me. I can't resist turning and kissing her coffee-flavored lips.

"We shouldn't do this," I murmur, kissing her again.

"Why not? We'll have all this food to sustain us."

"Because ..." I trail off as I hear car doors slamming, and voices raised in anticipation.

Brooke hastens to the window, which looks out to the front yard. "What the hell?"

I step behind her and motion the mob inside. I've left the front door unlocked for them.

"Good morning." Ryan leads the pack through the house to the kitchen. He waves a bottle of champagne. "Happy housewarming!"

He's followed by Calandra then Ben and Zach with their ladies. My mom and dad enter with Great Aunt Mary and Andrew, and then Viola and Craig Marsh, and Cedric.

"Great house, sis," Cedric booms. "Happy house-warming."

"How did you all even know I'd accept it?" Brooke says, eyes shining. She's overwhelmed by the gift baskets, hugs, and kisses.

"We didn't," Cedric answers. "Austin said he'd warn us off if you told him to go fly a kite. He didn't say a word, so we figured you loved the place, and we're here."

"This is crazy." Brooke turns to me. "Something only you would do."

"That's me. Ca-razy." I turn back to the stove and start serving up food. "There's not a lot of furniture, so you'll all have to eat wherever you can find a spot. Calandra gets a chair."

"I'm pregnant, not feeble," Calandra says, but Ryan pulls out a kitchen chair and makes sure Calandra sits.

Brooke hugs Calandra. "Thank you, sweetie. I know you are responsible for me being able to clean up and wear the right clothes."

Brooke's not ashamed that everyone knows she and I spent the night together. She rolls with things like that, another trait of hers I love.

Zach and Abby make mimosas with the champagne and hand them out. I serve the food, and we break into groups to eat, sitting on floors, on the stairs, on the patio—it's cool in the shade this morning. Everyone praises my cooking, but I think they're mellowed by the mimosas. I'm a functional chef, not an innovative one.

Calandra and Brooke discuss what kind of furniture she can put in the house, and the two vow to go shopping together. Brooke says she'll trash all her old stuff or donate it to charity.

She seems relieved, and not certain why she's lived in her rundown house for so long. She hadn't paid attention to it, I knew. She could have afforded a beautiful condo or bigger house on her own, but she'd not taken the time or trouble.

Now she's an excited new homeowner. I'm glad I can give her something from my heart. Ryan was right about matching the grand gesture to what Brooke needed.

Not that I'm finished. I carry my dishes to the sink and start soaking them. I'll clean up in here so Brooke, the queen of the day, won't have to.

I step out to the patio where she's deep into an animated conversation with my mom and hers. I interrupt, take her by the hand, and lead her to the center of the yard, among the colorful plants that Abby had said were the right touch.

I wave for attention. "Thanks everyone for coming." I wait for the stragglers to emerge from the house, interested in what I'm doing. I raise Brooke's hand. She's self-conscious but doesn't pull away. "Let's hear it for Brooke and her beautiful abode."

Mimosa glasses are raised. "To Brooke and her beautiful abode?" Voices tumble over one another, and there's laughter and glass-clinking.

"One more thing." I swallow, my throat tight. "I'm not sure what Brooke will think of this, but you know me. I never say never."

Before Brooke can ask what the hell I'm talking about, I sink to one knee.

She drags in a breath. "Austin. What ...?"

The others try to quiet themselves, but there's much murmuring followed by *Shh, shh, shh* from others. It takes a while for them to settle down. Meanwhile, Brooke is staring at me from wide, beautiful dark eyes, her face creased with shock.

"You have a great new life," I say, taking Brooke's

stiff hands. "You own your own business, and now, this spectacular house." Chuckles float from the porch. "Would you consider adding one more new thing? A husband? I mean me," I clarify quickly.

"I—" Brooke eyes me wildly, her lips parted.

"No, let me finish this the right way." I clear my throat and speak so all our family and friends can hear me. "Brooke Marsh, will you marry me?"

———

Brooke

HE'S SERIOUS. I GAZE DOWN AT AUSTIN, THE MAN I love, with his generous heart and amazing smiles. I think of all we've been through, and what we've survived. It has always been Austin for me, no matter what, whether we were tight together or nearly two years apart.

I feel the smile spread across my face. "Yes," I say, then I shout it to the crowd on the porch. "Yes!"

Austin's on his feet, kissing me, arms around me. "Are you sure?"

"Yes," I say again, laughter on my lips as my family and my best friends surge around us. "I never say never."

"Neither of us do."

"How about I say I love you instead?" I ask, my whole body trembling in newfound happiness.

"Suits me."

Austin holds me, and though family and friends have joined us, we might be the only two people on the planet.

"I love you, Austin McLaughlin," I whisper so only he can hear.

"I love you, Brooke Marsh."

As Austin kisses me, our families tease the hell out of us and toast us, which is fine with me. I'm surrounded by love and laughter, and know I'm exactly where I belong.

Epilogue

Seven months later

Ryan

AS I LOOK into my daughter's eyes, I know the most precious thing in my life is in my arms. She's so like Calandra that her face blurs a few seconds, and my breath catches.

Calandra's watching me from the hospital bed, her dark hair disheveled, a smile wide on her tired face.

"Hello, Tara," I say to my daughter. I swear Tara burbles at me, knowing I'm her proud papa.

"We did it," Calandra whispers.

"*You* did it." I can't believe her strength and her courage. "I about passed out three times."

"I did it, because I had you next to me." Calandra reaches for my hand, grasping it with plenty of strength.

Calandra's tucked in bed, and Tara is with us. Soon the rest of the family will come in and meet our daughter, but right now, it's just the three of us.

When I think how close Calandra and I came to not being together at all, I shudder and hold Tara closer. How could I ever contemplate *not* being with Calandra, and not having the chance to cradle this beautiful child in my arms?

My family thinks they know the whole story but they don't. Only Calandra and I do. One day we'll tell Tara, but for now, Calandra and I alone share the tale.

I glance at Calandra, and her smile deepens as though she reads my thoughts. She's always understood everything about me, all the way back to when we were kids.

I carefully hand Tara to Calandra, already terrified I'll drop her. Calandra takes our daughter and snuggles her with confidence.

Tara is hungry—I'll come to know that *Dad, I'm hungry,* will flow from her lips throughout her busy childhood—and Calandra moves her gown so Tara can feed.

It's a beautiful moment, mother and child, and me watching over them.

When Tara finishes—for now—I kiss Calandra's lips and then Tara's downy head.

"Love you," I say softly. "Both of you. I can't tell you how much."

"I know." Calandra kisses me in return. "Because I feel the same." She glances at the door. My family and hers is hovering, waiting with excited anticipation. "Should we let them in?"

"Sure," I say. "Let's put them out of their misery. But first ..." I give my wife another long kiss until Tara blurts a sound that draws our attention to her again. Smart girl.

"Thank you, Calandra," I murmur.

"For going through labor?" She grins. "Sure, no problem."

"For sticking with me." I touch her hair, brush her cheek with the back of my hand. "For giving me a chance."

"For giving you a night," Calandra says, her smile impish. "And what a night."

It had been. Damn, it was the best. But it couldn't compare to living with Calandra this past year, and *nothing* can top today.

We exchange one more kiss, then I stride to the door and throw it open, admitting Tara's uncles, aunts, and grandparents, who will spoil the hell out of our daughter for the next twenty years.

THANK YOU FOR READING! THE STORY OF HOW Calandra and Ryan come together is told in *Give Me One Night*, Book 4 of the McLaughlin Brothers.

Also by Jennifer Ashley

The McLaughlin Brothers

(Contemporary Romance)

This Changes Everything

Why Don't You Stay? ... Forever

Never Say Never

Give Me One Night

Riding Hard

(Contemporary Romance)

Adam

Grant

Carter

Tyler

Ross

Kyle

Ray

Snowbound in Starlight Bend

Shifters Unbound

(paranormal romance)

Pride Mates

Primal Bonds

Bodyguard

Wild Cat

Hard Mated

Mate Claimed

"Perfect Mate" (novella)

Lone Wolf

Tiger Magic

Feral Heat

Wild Wolf

Bear Attraction

Mate Bond

Lion Eyes

Bad Wolf

Wild Things

White Tiger

Guardian's Mate

Red Wolf

Midnight Wolf

Tiger Striped

A Shifter Christmas Carol

Iron Master

The Last Warrior

Shifter Made ("Prequel" short story)

The Mackenzies Series

(Historical Romance)

The Madness of Lord Ian Mackenzie

Lady Isabella's Scandalous Marriage

The Many Sins of Lord Cameron

The Duke's Perfect Wife

A Mackenzie Family Christmas: The Perfect Gift

The Seduction of Elliot McBride

The Untamed Mackenzie

The Wicked Deeds of Daniel Mackenzie

Scandal and the Duchess

Rules for a Proper Governess

The Stolen Mackenzie Bride

A Mackenzie Clan Gathering

Alec Mackenzie's Art of Seduction

The Devilish Lord Will

A Rogue Meets a Scandalous Lady

A Mackenzie Yuletide

(in print in A Mackenzie Clan Christmas)

Stormwalker

(w/a Allyson James)

Stormwalker

Firewalker

Shadow Walker

"Double Hexed"

Nightwalker

Dreamwalker

Dragon Bites

Kat Holloway "Below Stairs" Victorian Mysteries

A Soupçon of Poison

Death Below Stairs

Scandal Above Stairs

Death in Kew Gardens

Murder in the East End

Death at the Crystal Palace

About the Author

New York Times bestselling and award-winning author Jennifer Ashley has written more than 100 published novels and novellas in romance, urban fantasy, mystery, and historical fiction under the names Jennifer Ashley, Allyson James, and Ashley Gardner. Jennifer's books have been translated into more than a dozen languages and have earned starred reviews in *Publisher's Weekly* and *Booklist*. When she isn't writing, Jennifer enjoys playing music (guitar, piano, flute), reading, hiking, and building dollhouse miniatures.

More about Jennifer's books can be found at http://www.jenniferashley.com

To keep up to date on her new releases, join her newsletter here:

http://eepurl.com/47kLL

www.ingramcontent.com/pod-product-compliance
Lightning Source LLC
Chambersburg PA
CBHW032033180726

48284CB00008B/2576